Hope

by

Robert K. Swisher Jr.

Text copyright © 2004 Robert K. Swisher Jr.

OPEN TALON PRESS

**PUBLISHED BY
OPEN TALON PRESS**

EDITORS: Sheila Awalt

COVER DESIGNER: Samantha Fury
PRINT FORMAT: Samantha Fury

Library of Congress - In Publication Date

Swisher, Robert K, 1947 -
HOPE: A novel / by Robert K. Swisher Jr.
Summary: love, fantasy, longing, hope, old age
ISBN: 978-0-578-94081-6
LCN: 20211913111

OTHER PUBLISHED NOVELS BY ROBERT K. SWISHER JR.

Historical Fiction: Trade and E-book
Published by Sunstone Press
The Land
Fatal Destiny

Contemporary Western Fiction: Trade and E-book
PUBLISHED BY SUNSTONE PRESS
How Far the Mountain
The Last Narrow Gauge Train Robbery
The Last Day in Paradise
Love Lies Bleeding
The Man From the Mountain

Literary: Out of Print
Published by Samisdat Press - Canada
American Love Story

Young Adult: Trade Only
Published by Echo Press California
The Weaver
Published by Sunstone Press
Only Magic

Humor: E-book and Trade
Conversations With the Golf God

Mystery Series: E-book and Trade
Bob Roosevelt Mystery Series – 4 novels

Contemporary Fiction: E-book and Trade
Hope
A Circle Around Forever

Trade and E-book
Published by Open Talon Press
Vent
Grammar Nazis Are Not Always Rite, Right, Write
Vent Revisited
The Lonely Cowboy
How Bridge McCoy Learned to Say I Love you
Short stories and poetry in literary journals, articles in outdoor magazines.
Reviews by Publishers Weekly, Best Sellers, Library Journal, and many
others.

Hope

Dedication:

There is a place beyond dreams for only those who dare to fly

Chapter One

"It is always the same," Martha Dearheart muttered to herself, looking disdainfully at the lunch tray in front of her. She then made a dour face. Although she liked baked chicken, she despised peas, which seemed to be the focal point of her lunch, and she also loathed watery mashed potatoes. Taking a deep breath she pushed the tray away and marched defiantly out of the dining room.

An aide, wondering if he should try and stop Martha, looked beseechingly at Nurse Steal. Nurse Steal shook her head and smiled understandingly at Martha Dearheart's back. Several of the other residents wanted to follow Martha, but they did not have her inner strength or resolve.

Martha Dearheart made her way slowly down the east hall. For being eighty-two she was in reasonable health. Her arthritis was tolerable. She did not need a cane or walker. She only took one pill for high blood pressure and she did not really give a hoot about her cholesterol. Her complexion was rosy and she did not dye her short, gray, curly hair. Her green eyes, though intense, did not completely hide a deep sadness that had been her companion for many years. Her husband had called her his gentle bulldog and in truth she had many features of one. She was short and frumpy, with strong arms and legs, and radiated an inner strength that made people rely on her.

Passing the open doors to the resident's rooms Martha felt perturbed. It was a rule at Rest View the doors could not be completely closed, something about speed of access if there was an emergency. Martha Dearheart thought it was a stupid rule. What was an extra minute or two before death? Rest View was not a young folk's home. It was a home for old people. Old people are supposed to die, but she felt they should have the right to die in privacy. "I should form an action committee and try to change a few things around here. We are not prisoners," she said angrily.

Martha Dearheart stopped by the door to Bertha Shields' room. Ninety-three year old Bertha was in bed. The skin on her face folded over her bones like fine linen paper. The veins in her arms protruded a dark blue as if they were a road map to a distant land that only existed in dreams. A few wisps of white hair grew from her pink scalp. She was singing a lullaby to a light brown teddy bear she cradled in her arms. The teddy bear was worn and ragged as if it had been the companion for several generations of rough and tumble children.

"Bertha," Martha Dearheart called gently.

Bertha Shields did not stop singing.

"Bertha," Martha Dearheart called louder.

Bertha Shields stopped singing, but did not look at Martha Dearheart. After a long pause, as if she had to weigh each word before she could speak, she said in a raspy voice, "Leave us alone, can't you see Randolph and I are resting?"

"I was just wondering how Randolph was doing?" Martha Dearheart asked with deep concern in her voice.

"He still has a cold," Bertha Shields replied. "You know how these springtime colds can hang on."

"Well, I hope he gets over it soon. I don't want you to catch it," Martha Dearheart said before leaving.

Bertha Shields held a Kleenex under the nose of the teddy

bear. "If people would let us rest you would get over your cold," she said tenderly.

The black glossy eyes of the teddy bear stared vacantly back at her as she kissed the tip of its nose.

Martha Dearheart went to her room. She felt she had the best room at Rest View. From her window she could look out over a rolling hill. The hill was now turning green after the long dreary winter, as were the oak and cottonwood trees at its base. Next to the cottonwood trees was a marshy area where cattails would soon begin to sprout and the red and yellow winged blackbirds would arrive with their happy carefree songs. "At least I did not die during the winter," she said with a trace of victory in her voice. Although she did not fear dying, she did not want to die during the winter. She wanted to be placed in the earth when it was warm and filled with the promise of young life. But, no matter her wishes, she felt she would die during the winter, figuring it would be another of life's sardonic twists.

Glancing at the photographs of her husband and son hanging on the wall a dart of sadness tried to enter her heart, but she quelled it. At times the memories of them were more like dreams only partially remembered - bits and fragments that made no sense. But at other times she could remember aspects of their lives together in vivid detail like years were no more than seconds.

Martha Dearheart removed her shoes, rubbed her swollen feet and reclined on the bed. "I am always so weary," she sighed, "so weary and useless. Life is such a routine that the days mean nothing. Monday could be Thursday or Tuesday could be Sunday. We all need some excitement around here."

She looked at the electric clock. They were all going to gather in the dayroom at two. "You must not nap so long that you will have to rush to get ready," she told herself before shutting her eyes and pondering if she would wear the small garnet pin her husband had given her or the pearl pin her son had given her when he was back home for the last time.

Hope

******

Nurse Steal, dressed in a starched white uniform, gazed warmly at the residents. She was a large big boned woman, close to two hundred pounds, with close cropped brown hair and soft caring eyes that at times could be blue or green. She was only fifty-two years old, but most of the time she felt closer to seventy. Nurse Steal inwardly sighed - all of the nineteen people in the dining room except Harold seemed to be lost and lonely puppets that could care less if the puppet master ever wanted to pull their strings again. Harold was by the window, flapping his arms like he was trying to fly, and happily watching two spring robins as they hopped around the yard searching for unsuspecting worms.

"It is naptime," Nurse Steal announced. "I don't want to hear any talking, no radios or TV's. It is important you get your rest."

Several aides, wearing blue uniforms that reminded the residents of pajamas, pushed the wheelchair bound people to their rooms. Other residents shuffled down the hall in their individual modes of movement, some with walkers, some with canes, some with small delicate steps followed by a few quick jerky steps before having to grab the handrail that ran the length of the hall. "Harold good boy," Harold said to Nurse Steal as he shuffled by.

Nurse Steal smiled warmly at him.

When the dining room was empty, Nurse Steal grimaced at the hundreds of peas that were scattered all over the floor. "I hate peas," she commented distastefully, remembering how her mother used to make her eat all her peas.

Down the hall the janitor was getting his mop and bucket out of the closet. "You cannot scrub death away," Nurse Steal said, and feeling like a warden of a prison she started her rounds to make sure the residents were taking their naps. She prayed she would not have to call an ambulance. It had been three days since the last death. The record was one hundred and five days without a death. But even if there was only one death a year, it was too many. Each death ripped a small piece out of Nurse Steal's large and caring heart.

******

Nurse Steal stopped by Harold's door and peeked in. Her routine for the past nine years had not changed. After making sure the residents were resting she went to the nurses' station, did her necessary paperwork, made sure patients who were on medication had been given their pills, drank a cup of decaffeinated coffee, and went to Harold's room.

Harold lay on top of the covers, looking out the window and did not see Nurse Steal. Nurse Steal held a deep empathy for all the people at Rest View, but Harold was a cherished portion of her heart - a portion she would not shut off from all the sadness she felt around her. She called it her tear filled with love.

Harold was not old in comparison to the other residents. He was only forty-eight. He was tall, medium built and weighed about 150 pounds, with shoulder length white hair that he seldom combed, but somehow was always neat. His back was slightly deformed, making him walk with his head stuck out in front of him like a whooping crane and gave the impression he was always off balance. He also dragged his left foot slightly, so his walk was more of a shuffle. When he got in a hurry he skipped. His face was oval and radiated like a happy jack-o-lantern whose only purpose was to make children smile. He had three outfits of clothes, all the same: blue bib overalls, white T-shirts, and red high-topped tennis shoes, which he was always being reminded to tie. Harold was in Rest View because he was simple. Some god, or demon, or something in his system had decided that the mind of a six year old was going to be enough for Harold. After being abandoned by his parents, he spent his young life being shuffled from one orphanage to another until as an adult he became a ward of the state. He would live out his remaining days at Rest View. He did not speak well, but he could communicate in slow jerky sentences that seemed to require all of his energy to express.

Even though Harold had never had a family life, he was not bitter or angry. He smiled all the time, but underneath the smile people knew he carried a deep sadness that would never go away.

Pulling his right thumb out of his mouth Harold coughed, and put his thumb back into his mouth. On a small redbud tree, not five yards from his window, two gray sparrows darted from branch to branch. Harold, pointing with his free hand, said in a childlike voice, "Bird, bird, pretty bird."

Nurse Steal's eyes softened as she looked at Harold's back. She knew he had his thumb in his mouth. When she had first taken the job as head nurse the other nurses were trying to stop Harold from sucking on his thumb. Nurse Steal put a quick end to their efforts. "Leave the poor man alone. He has to have one pleasure in life," she sternly informed them.

Nurse Steal sat on the edge of the bed. Rolling his head sideways Harold smiled fondly at her. He had light blue eyes, eyes the color of a fall Colorado sky - eyes that to Nurse Steal held all the intelligence in the world, but the intelligence was trapped inside of Harold and could not get out. "Bird," Harold said, taking his thumb out of his mouth and pointing at the redbud tree.

"Yes Harold, two beautiful birds," Nurse Steal said sounding like a mother talking to a young child.

"Birds fly," Harold said like it was the greatest truth of all time.

Nurse Steal gently brushed Harold's hair off of his forehead. "Yes," she said softly. "The birds fly."

Harold started to put his thumb back in his mouth but he stopped. "I fly. I fly like birds," he said nodding his head.

"Yes, I know you can fly," Nurse Steal said with a deeply saddened heart, knowing flying was merely a simple dream. And what is a dream? Is it nothing but a figment of hope that can never come true? Nurse Steal's dreams had never come true. She had always been big and plain. When she was in school she was never asked out on dates and as a woman no man had ever loved her. Her life was a constant fight with loneliness. She longed desperately to be loved and caressed. To have a person in her life she could share things with, but now it seemed out of reach and at times not worth the effort. "You get some rest," she said tenderly.

After Nurse Steal left Harold got out of bed and peered through the window. The movement startled two sparrows and they darted away, which caused Harold to giggle.

Harold held his arms out away from his body and started flapping them as though they were wings. "I fly, I fly," he said happily. "I fly."

Rose Merrywood, whose room was across the hall from Harold's listened intently to Harold and murmured, "Fly away Harold, for all of us please fly."

Harold stopped flapping his arms and put his face against the window, trying to see if there were any more birds. But he could not see any. "I fly," he said quietly like a little boy with a secret. "I fly like birds."

******

A bird singing "Fa, La, La," woke Harold up. Tip-toeing to the door he peered secretively up and down the hall, no one was about and it was as quiet as a secluded meadow. He tip-toed to the window and there was a small, drab, brown bird in the red bud tree. The only thing remarkable about the bird was its eyes. The eyes were vivid red and seemed to possess a mysterious knowledge that was beyond the comprehension of all other creatures. "Fa, La, La," the bird sang.

Harold cupped his hand behind his ear. "Fa, La, La," the bird sang again.

"Bird, bird," he whispered and opened the window the few inches it would open. The windows only opened a slight amount in fear a resident might try and leave without permission.

"Fa, La, La," the bird beckoned.

Standing as straight as he could Harold started flapping his arms.

"Fa, La, La," the bird sang.

Harold flapped his arms faster. "Fa, La, La," the bird sang once more.

Harold slowed down his flapping and sang in a whisper, "Fa, La, La, Fa, La, La."

Slowly, Harold's feet came off the ground - first a quarter of an inch, then a half an inch, then a complete inch. Harold sped up his flapping and his feet rose over a foot from the floor. Shutting his eyes he flapped faster and he was suddenly transformed into a small brown bird with a tiny splash of blue on its breast. Quicker than a blink he flew out the window. He flew away from town and Rest View. He flew over trees and soared high above the clouds where only the endless blue sky filled his vision. He sailed over a large lake and dipped down and sped barely over the surface of the water. "Fa, La, La, Fa, La, La," he sang in rapture and shut his eyes. The air rushed over him and his heart seemed to overflow with all the joy in the world.

Harold's feet touched the floor. Opening his eyes he let his arms fall to his sides and listened for the bird. There was only silence. Shutting the window he tip-toed toward his bed. "I fly, I fly, Harold good boy. Nurse Steal fly too. Harold love Nurse Steal," he said.

Across the hall Rose Merrywood smiled.

Chapter Two

Martha Dearheart decided she would wear the pearl pin her son had given her for the gathering in the dayroom. She looked fondly at the unadorned white pine jewelry box on top of her dresser. It was a gift from her long deceased husband when they were first dating and to her it was more beautiful than a gilded treasure chest. Opening the jewelry box she gently picked up a pearl pin as if it was as delicate as a hummingbird's egg. The pin was one large single pearl set in a gold mount. She pinned it on the collar of her blue dress. Her son had been proud when he had given her the pin. She had also been proud. Proud he was in the Navy. "You be careful," she told him as he boarded the plane that would take him back to Seattle after his leave, trying her best not to show her fear or cry.

"Mom," he had said fearlessly. "People in the Navy don't get killed in a war, that's the job of the Army and the Marines."

She had never seen her son again. In 1969 the gun ship he was on hit a mine while patrolling the Mekong River in Vietnam and his body was blown into little pieces. What remained of him they had cremated and scattered the ashes by his favorite fishing spot along Grand River. She rubbed the pin tenderly, no longer overcome with grief, but there was always a hollow spot in the corner of her heart that no amount of time would ever take away. "You made me strong," she said as she left her room. "Something I never really wanted."

Martha Dearheart started for the dayroom. She could smell the odor of polish and disinfectant the janitor had buffed into the white linoleum floor during their nap. Everything was polished and disinfected in Rest View. The walls were oyster white and spotless. The windows always clean. The tabletops were clean enough one did not really need a tray to eat. The only carpet was in the day room. There were framed prints on the walls of farm houses and landscapes that were devoid of life or any form of emotion. Martha felt like she lived in a lab. She was a mouse that nurses in starched white uniforms made notes about and conducted experiments on to see how old people reacted to being overly clean. "I really do have to start a committee and demand some changes around here," she said resolutely to herself. But she wondered if the other residents were brave enough to back her. Most of them moved through each day like robots trying to remember feelings that were hiding outside the walls of Rest View.

Martha Dearheart passed bravely by the nurses' station in the dayroom. She knew she was out of her room early but did not care. "I see you have your lovely pearl pin on, the one your son gave you," Nurse Steal said, never one to enforce rules she did not believe in.

"At times I think a pearl holds all the secrets of the world," Martha Dearheart replied.

"Maybe one day we will discover how to find them," Nurse Steal said wishfully.

The dayroom was a large room. There were many windows with blinds that when partially open the room seemed muted and slightly out of kilter. When the blinds were completely open the light to the residents was like a hug from a dear friend. In one corner of the room was a large screen TV, with chairs and sofas placed in front of it. In another corner were two sofas with a large magazine rack between them. The magazines ranged from *Home and Garden* to *Outdoor Life*. Mr. Fist had tried to have Rest

View order *Playboy*. But Mr. Dry, the Director of Rest View, said it was against Rest View's moral character and would not allow it. He did inform Mr. Fist he could have a subscription, but he could never take the magazine out of his room. It was a nice gesture, but since Mr. Fist and his three friends only received fifty dollars a month they could not afford a subscription - the rest of their money went to Rest View.

Mr. Fist, after being told, cursed, "He must have never slept with a woman."

His buddies that Mr. Fist described photographs of women to from the available magazines because they could no longer see well enough echoed his thoughts.

In the center of the dayroom were more tables and chairs, and one table covered with various games and decks of cards. In a third corner was a small, slightly out of tune piano. Directly centered in the middle of the west wall was the nurses' station which was nick named, **"Big Brother"** by the residents. What bothered Martha about the dayroom were the artificial plants scattered about. Plants should be real, filled with the promise of life. Plants should need care and bloom. Fake plants were like all the residents, always the same, no change, no dreams to grow, merely the same color day to day, year to year, until out of boredom they were discarded.

Martha Dearheart sat at a round table that was in front of a large picture window. She could see the yet unplanted flowerbed outside the window. For a moment she thought of all the lovely flowers she used to have around her home - the peonies, the daisies, the red and yellow roses. The clematis that crept around the porch each summer until it erupted into a profusion of lapis blue flowers. Starting to feel sad she drove the thought of home from her mind. Like all the people in Rest View she would never have a home again. Home was a faded dream or at times a nightmare. She turned from the window as an aide wheeled the frail Rose Merrywood to the table.

Rose Merrywood was ninety-one and had been confined to a wheelchair for over ten years. Rose's features were soft and sagging and her arms and hands had little strength, although she could feed herself. She always wore a sack dress with a flower print and kept her white hair tightly permed. Over her useless legs was spread a baby blue Afghan. "We lived through another nap," Rose Merrywood said to Martha Dearheart after the aide left.

"Too bad, isn't it?" Martha Dearheart replied, but not grimly.

"Yes it is," Rose Merrywood agreed.

Martha Dearheart touched the pearl pin on her collar. The pin seemed to radiate warmth as though a portion of the sun was trapped inside the milky white drop.

"The aides made me eat my peas at lunch," Rose Merrywood announced, making a face like she had just sucked on a lemon.

"Next time, you just spit them on the floor," Martha Dearheart ordered.

"Oh, I couldn't do that," Rose Merrywood stated.

"It is people who don't protest that stop change," Martha Dearheart said, sounding annoyed.

"No, it is not," Rose Merrywood replied meekly.

"You, being a schoolteacher, were never trained to cause change. You were trained to spit out facts and make sure your pupils became clones to the system," Martha Dearheart said, but not in a caustic way.

"Everybody can't be a brave rebel like you," Rose Merrywood answered. "And besides, we have been through this before."

Martha Dearheart had been a reporter for a medium sized newspaper and had tried her best to uncover corruption and anything that was not right. She had always been an advocate for the small people in life - the unfortunate people born with no luck or promise that society normally blamed for all its faults.

"Look, a butterfly," Martha Dearheart said excitedly, pointing out the window.

Rose Merrywood looked quickly, but the butterfly was gone. "Was it a monarch?" she asked.

"Yes, I believe it was," Martha Dearheart replied, "even

though it is early for monarchs to be in our area."

"Oh, dear, I wish I had seen it," Rose Merrywood said sadly.

A loud noise shrieked through the dayroom, but as quickly as it sounded, it ceased. Both Martha and Rose grimaced. The front door was equipped with a buzzer. When it was opened from either side the buzzer rang sharply and was only turned off with a button at the nurses' station. Its purpose was to let staff members know when a resident went outside when he or she was not supposed to. Residents could only go outside if accompanied by an aide or a nurse or if they checked in with the nurses' station. Most did not bother to go outside except the few residents that smoked. "It's a dreadful sound," Rose Merrywood said. "It reminds me of those silly war movies when the submarine has to dive to try and escape from an enemy destroyer dropping depth charges."

"It is a dreadful sound that should not be associated with this place," Martha Dearheart said.

Grace Brethren, with the aid of an aluminum walker, made her way slowly but steadily toward the table. Eighty-four year old Grace Brethren was tall and thin with a sharply chiseled face. Her lips were tight lines that seldom smiled. She always wore dark clothes and kept her long white hair rolled into a tight bun. She wore no jewelry or makeup. She had never married and did not tell anyone what she had done during her life. She reminded Martha Dearheart of a spinster schoolteacher who had taught at an old fashioned all girl's school run by a strict religious sect. Rose Merrywood smiled at Grace Brethren. "Martha saw a beautiful monarch butterfly," she said. "But I did not see it."

"It was God's will," Grace Brethren replied sternly.

Although neither Martha Dearheart nor Rose Merrywood was deeply religious, they were not sinners by any means. To the people of Rest View, Grace Brethren had enough religion for all of them. If there were a person who would gain sainthood it would be Grace Brethren. To her there was nothing in life but prayer and the total disregard for anything that might prove to be joyful or pleasurable, either of which would send one's soul on a downward plunge into the depths of evil that could never be corrected, no matter what penance the sinner would offer up for his or her redemption. To Grace Brethren there was not a person in Rest View who had even the slightest chance of seeing the pearly gates.

"How is God?" Martha Dearheart asked Grace Brethren, winking at Rose Merrywood.

Rose Merrywood covered her smile with her small bent hand.

Grace Brethren, never one to fluster in the presence of sinners, shook off the question in her usual stern and pious manner. "Did you really see a butterfly?" she asked.

"It might have been a monarch," Martha Dearheart said.

"It was," Rose Merrywood said.

"You didn't even see it," Martha Dearheart said.

"You would never lie," Rose Merrywood said.

"No matter what it was, moth or butterfly, it was God's will," Grace Brethren said.

Martha Dearheart shook her head in disbelief.

Mr. Fist shuffled into the dayroom. Martha Dearheart swore she could see the sunlight pass through his frail body. All three ladies seeing Mr. Fist quickly turned their heads toward the window. Only Rose Merrywood hoped he would stop at the table.

Mr. Fist approached the table. "What three beautiful flowers from the valley of life are placed before me," he said.

"Oh, Mr. Fist," Rose Merrywood gushed.

Grace Brethren huffed and glared disapprovingly at Rose Merrywood.

"Mr. Fist, stuff it," Martha Dearheart said.

"You have such charm, such simplicity of word, such a flair for the dramatic," Mr. Fist grinned, not feeling the small droplet of spit that gathered at the corner of his mouth.

"Go play with the boys," Grace Brethren said stiffly. "It is spring and we ladies would like to be left alone to enjoy the view."

"Until the dark then, my lovelies," Mr. Fist said. "Until you once again turn back your perfumed sheets for me I will bid you farewell and return to my lowly magazine pages, knowing that the photographs of women do not compare to the three beauties I now feast my eyes upon." With that Mr. Fist bowed and shuffled toward the magazine rack.

"Dear God," Grace Brethren said. "Even old men only think about our bodies."

"I like men to think about my body," Rose Merrywood said. "My husband was a very passionate man."

"With seven children, your husband was always in rut," Martha Dearheart said with a smile.

"Jealous," Rose Merrywood replied with a twinkle in her eye.

"I bet in his day Mr. Fist was quite the ladies man," Martha Dearheart said.

"He was a heathen, just like he is now," Grace Brethren said. "A heathen who probably spent his life hanging out in the bars and dancing with any loose woman he could find."

"I loved to dance," Rose Merrywood said, looking sadly at her shriveled legs, adding, "and for your knowledge Mr. Fist owned a bar."

"I figured as much," Grace Brethren said.

"I bet you never once in your life danced all night," Rose Merrywood said. "Danced and then sat with your love and looked at the moon and the stars. Maybe then you would truly know God?"

"God doesn't dance, nor does he sit idly under trees," Grace Brethren said.

"Pity," Martha Dearheart said.

The dayroom was beginning to fill with people. An aide wheeled Bertha Shields and Randolph in front of the TV. Sesame Street was about to start and everybody knew Randolph loved Sesame Street. According to Bertha Shields Randolph was especially fond of the Cookie Monster.

Mr. Fist's three friends, Robert Begone, Jake Lost, and Paul Mouse, were all sitting on the sofa by the magazine rack waiting for Mr. Fist to describe a lady from one of the magazines.

Robert Begone was seventy-eight years old, bald, and

plump. He had been a long distance truck driver. As usual he had forgotten to put on one of his shoes which he always thought someone had stolen. He and Mr. Fist were constantly trying to escape Rest View and were in serious competition on how far they made it from the front door before they were captured by the aides. To Mr. Fist the idea of breaking out of Rest View was a compulsion that never left his mind.

Jake Lost looked like he had spent his eighty years riding freight trains. From the few stories he told about his life it seemed Jake Lost had been a jack of all trades - none of which he had ever really enjoyed, but he believed work was not supposed to be enjoyed. He was nearly deaf and was always fiddling with his hearing aid - it was either too low or too high.

Paul Mouse, befitting his name, was a small shriveled up ninety-year-old man who continually scratched different parts of his body. Paul Mouse had owned a shoe store. They had all been in Rest View for over six years, their wives were deceased, and their children were so scattered they seldom visited. They had not known each other during their 'real lives' as they called their days before Rest View.

Mr. Fist thumbed through a copy of *Better Homes and Gardens* trying to find a photograph of a woman he had not yet described to his buddies.

Mr. Fist began describing a beautiful young lady wearing a white bikini and holding a glass of orange juice. "Why does she need orange juice?" Paul Mouse asked, scratching his chest.

"She needs it to keep her lovers full of vigor," Robert Begone said.

"I wouldn't need vigor," Paul Mouse said scratching his arm.

"Talk louder," Jake Lost hollered fiddling with his hearing aid.

"I'll be damned," Robert Begone said, noticing he only had one shoe on. "Somebody stole my shoe while I've been sitting here."

"Would you guys shut up and listen," Mr. Fist said slightly exasperated.

******

When Harold woke from his nap, the first thing he did was look at the redbud tree, but there were no birds. His mouth was dry from falling asleep with his thumb in it and he was thirsty. He put on his tennis shoes without tying them and got a drink of water from the small sink in the corner of his room, setting the glass where Nurse Steal had showed him. "Good boy," he said, proud of his feat.

He then concentrated on tying the laces to his red high-topped tennis shoes. After a few minutes he managed to tie the laces in two loose bows. He felt happy. "Nurse Steal like," he beamed.

Harold did not head for the dayroom but shuffled toward the end of the hall. Rest View was constructed with the dayroom at the center. Off of the dayroom ran two wings where the resident's rooms were. Down a third wing, also off of the dayroom, were the dining room and the various offices and rooms where medications, linens, and such were stored. At the end of each wing where the residents lived were two windows and a double door. The doors were always locked, and the windows, like the windows in the resident's rooms, could only be opened a few inches. There were several chairs for people to sit when they wanted to be left alone.

As Harold came to the door of a room, he would stop and peer into the room without crossing the threshold of the door. Satisfied nobody was in the room, he would go to the next room. If a person was sleeping in their room, he would tip-toe up to the side of the bed and peer at them to make sure they were ok. If a person was awake he would say hello. At the end of the hall, he pushed on the locked doors and then gazed out the window. Several hundred yards away he saw the dark outline of three birds perched on a telephone wire. Pointing with his left hand he held up two fingers and said, "Birds, four birds."

He leaned forward until his forehead rested against the glass so he could see the birds closer. After the birds flew away he headed toward the dayroom.

By the nurses' station, Harold proudly showed Nurse Steal his tied shoes.

"That is very good, Harold," Nurse Steal said.

Harold grinned. "Birds gone," he said.

Taking a piece of butterscotch candy out of her purse she gave it to Harold.

"Thank you," Harold said shyly, putting the candy in his pocket.

Harold stopped by a table where George Early and Henry Right were playing their daily checker game. The men were in their seventies, wheelchair bound, and looked enough alike they could have been brothers, but they were not. Both men played serious checkers with the intent on crushing their opponent. Neither of the men looked at Harold. George Early jumped two of Henry Right's checkers. "Got your ass," George Early said with a wry grin.

"His ass," Harold chimed jumping up and down happily.

Henry Right scowled, contemplating the checkerboard. Harold looked at the board and also scowled, even though he had no idea how to play checkers. After several minutes, and Henry Right not deciding where to move, Harold went to visit Grace Brethren, Rose Merrywood, and Martha Dearheart.

"Hello," Harold said to the ladies in his childlike voice.

"You look well today, Harold," Martha Dearheart said.

"I fly," Harold answered.

"I bet it is wonderful to fly," Rose Merrywood said. "Fly and be able to see the earth from above the ground."

Harold stretched his arms straight out from his body and bent low as though he was soaring.

"I fly, I fly," he bubbled.

Martha Dearheart and Rose Merrywood laughed along with Harold.

Harold, with his arms outstretched, glided over to Bertha Shields and Randolph.

"You shouldn't do that to him," Grace Brethren scolded Martha Dearheart and Rose Merrywood. "He is a poor lost soul."

"The Indians believed the simple people were the closest to God," Rose Merrywood said.

"Simple people can sin," Grace Brethren said.

"If you do not know what you are doing, how can you sin?" Martha Dearheart asked.

"We are all born with sin on our soul," Grace Brethren said.

"I don't think so. A loving God would not curse us," Martha Dearheart said.

"Oh, look," Rose Merrywood said, pointing out the window. "There are two monarch butterflies."

"They are so lovely," Grace Brethren said.

"It would be nice to fly," Rose Merrywood said, looking at her withered legs. "But I would want to be a butterfly, fluttering through fields of clover and landing on all the dainty and wonderful flowers."

"I imagine you have spent most of your life fluttering along," Grace Brethren said piously.

Martha Dearheart shook her head sadly. "Grace, life is all merely fluttering around. No matter how you live, or how serious you are, it is all fluttering."

Grace Brethren shut her eyes and said a prayer for the people who could not see the light.

Harold sat on the sofa next to Bertha Shield's wheelchair. Randolph was perched on Bertha's knee with his glass eyes pointing directly at the TV.

"Hello," Harold said, putting his face right next to Randolph.

"Leave Randolph alone," Bertha Shields said crossly. "This is the only program he enjoys."

Harold sat back obediently. "Cookie Monster," he said with glee.

Bertha Shields held the teddy bear up. "Cookie Monster, Cookie Monster," she echoed.

"Four cookies," Harold said, counting with the Cookie Monster.

Mr. Fist closed the copy of *Better Homes and Gardens*. The four men sighed in unison. After a few moments of savoring Mr.

Fist's description of a girl dressed in a bra and lace panties, Robert Begone said, "I wish we could go fishing."

"I'd like to go fishing," Jake Lost said. "I used to fish all the time."

"You'd think they would take us fishing," Mr. Fist said. "All we do is sit around and do nothing."

"They are afraid we would feel alive," Jake Lost said.

Paul Mouse, without saying goodbye, headed to his room.

"Wonder what got into him?" Mr. Fist asked.

"Loneliness," Jake Lost said.

"Did either one of you guys take my shoe?" Robert Begone asked, looking at his feet.

"Your shoe is in your room," Mr. Fist said.

"Why would someone steal my shoe and then take it to my room?" Robert Begone asked feeling puzzled.

"People are weird," Mr. Fist said.

Mr. Fist made his way to where Martha Dearheart, Rose Merrywood, and Grace Brethren were gazing intently out the window hoping the butterflies would return.

"Your vision has never left my mind," Mr. Fist said to Rose Merrywood and then picked up her small bent hand and kissed it, leaving a small drop of spittle on her fingers. Bowing low, he winked at all the ladies and left.

Grace Brethren, in disgust, inched away from the table and clicked away in her walker without saying goodbye.

"I bet she never slept with a man," Rose Merrywood said.

"Only if they tied her up," Martha Dearheart replied.

Rose Merrywood waved at an aide who came over to push her back to her room.

Martha Dearheart took a deep breath. There are so many things that could be done around Rest View to not make us feel so alienated she thought as she went to her room. Two butterflies landed on the windowsill, unseen.

When Sesame Street was over Harold clapped.

"My, my, what a good show, Randolph," Bertha Shields said. "Didn't we learn something today?"

"One, two, three, four," Harold said, holding up three

fingers.

Nurse Steal came over. "Time for your medicine, Bertha," she said.

"I don't want it," Bertha Shields complained.

"I know, but Randolph wants you to take it," Nurse Steal said.

Nurse Steal pushed Bertha Shields to her room. Bertha Shields, clutching Randolph tightly to her chest, cried in protest, "I don't want to. I don't want to"

Harold went over to where George Early and Henry Right were still playing checkers. "I finally won one," Henry Right told Harold.

"Won," Harold said, holding up two fingers.

"Lucky bastard," George Early said angrily.

"Lucky bastard," Harold said.

"Lucky, my ass, I beat you fair and square," Henry Right retorted.

"My ass," Harold said.

A male aide came over to the checker table. "Time to get ready for supper," he said.

"Screw supper," Henry Right said.

"Screw supper," Harold said.

"Come on you three, finish this game up and then go and get ready. Tonight is bingo, you wouldn't want to be late for bingo," the aide said.

"Bingo sucks," George Early said.

"Sucks," Harold said.

The aide, exasperated, left.

"What do they think we are?" Henry Right asked disgustedly.

"Birds," Harold said.

"Yes, we are all a bunch of birds, but instead of being able to fly we are like chickens in a pen," George Early said.

"Fly, we fly," Harold said.

"I can't even walk. How do you expect me to fly?" George Early scowled.

Harold started flapping his arms.

Henry Right, in disgust, swept the checkers off of the board onto the floor. Harold jumped back in fear and wrapped his arms around his chest.

George Early and Henry Right gave each other a disgusted look and wheeled themselves toward their rooms. Nurse Steal began to pick up the checkers. Harold got down on his hands and knees and helped. "Thank you," Nurse Steal said.

After the checkers were picked up, Harold watched Nurse Steal straighten up the dayroom. Finished, she took Harold by the hand and walked with him to his room. "You wash your hands and get ready for supper," she told him.

Harold tilted his head and said, "It sucks."

"Yes, it all sucks," Nurse Steal replied.

After Nurse Steal left Harold put the piece of candy Nurse Steal had given to him in his drawer along with the fifty or sixty other pieces. "Harold is a good boy," he said. "But Harold not like butterscotch candy."

******

Martha Dearheart had changed clothes for supper. She was now wearing a green dress with a white belt and black shoes. She did not put either the garnet pin or the pearl pin on. She was in the dining room, the first to arrive as usual, and watched as the residents slowly made their way in for dinner. She was sad for a moment. Everyone looked lost - lost in a world where no dreams for the future could exist.

A young aide named Hazel was serving the food. Hazel was taking classes to become a registered nurse. Martha Dearheart and Hazel were good friends, and Hazel confided in her many times. Hazel was a small person and reminded Martha of a pixie. She had large brown eyes, an up turned nose, and parted her short auburn hair like a man. Hazel had been married at eighteen, given birth to a baby boy when she was twenty-one, and now at twenty-four was divorced and living with her parents. Even though Hazel always seemed happy and had a smile for everyone, Martha Dearheart could feel the loneliness she kept hidden. It seemed to Martha Dearheart that so many young people were lost, and even though she was old, she would not want to be young in the modern world.

Hazel placed a tray in front of Martha Dearheart. "It doesn't look too bad tonight," she said.

Martha Dearheart examined the broiled fish, cottage cheese and small tomato-less salad, and made a wry face. "At least there are no peas," she commented dryly.

Hazel smiled a knowing smile and set a tray down before Rose Merrywood. "Oh, good," Rose Merrywood said, "I love fish."

"If they would let us we could catch good fish for everybody," Mr. Fist said. "Not this broiled down tasteless cardboard they try to pass off as fish.

"Damn right," Robert Begone agreed.

"Where are your shoes?" Hazel asked Robert Begone.

Robert Begone looked at his feet. "Who stole my shoes?" he demanded and glared menacingly around the room.

Grace Brethren examined her food, made the sign of the cross, shut her eyes and said a prayer.

"Come over here and pray over my slop," Paul Mouse said to Grace Brethren. "Pray it doesn't kill me before my time."

George Early, having been a military man, gulped his food. "Eat your food and shut up," he growled to Paul Mouse.

"You tell him," Grace Brethren said. "He should be thankful he is able to eat and not some poor old man living on the street and starving to death."

"I am starving to death," Paul Mouse retorted.

Nurse Steal listened to the battering and was relieved when everybody finally began to eat. More than once she had asked Mr. Dry if they could take the residents out to eat at one of the restaurants in town. But Mr. Dry, in his normal seemingly uncaring and business-like manner, had always quoted some insurance regulation that if anything happened they could be sued for more money than the Federal Reserve was worth. Nurse Steal hoped Mr. Dry lived to be one hundred and twenty-five years old and had to spend fifty years of his life in an old folk's home like Rest View. And hopefully, God willing, she was the nurse in charge of his wing. But, Nurse Steal also knew Mr. Dry was under great pressure from the board of directors of the Rest View chain, and he did the best that he could. She did not envy him his position.

Bertha Shields cut her fish into tiny pieces and blew on them before holding a bite up for Randolph. "Isn't it good?" she cooed to the teddy bear before taking the bite herself.

"Give my fish to Randolph," Henry Right said. "He looks like he needs a little fattening up."

Harold, looking forlorn, pushed his food around on the tray. "Don't you like your food?" Nurse Steal asked him.

"No peas," Harold said.

"You eat everything on your plate, Harold," Martha Dearheart said, smiling at Nurse Steal. "And whenever we have peas Rose Merrywood and I will give you ours."

Harold grinned and began to eat.

When everyone was done the trays were cleared away and everyone was given a cookie and an orange flavored high vitamin protein drink. "I'd like a beer," Mr. Fist said to Grace Brethren. Alcohol, unless approved by a relative, was forbidden at Rest View, and unfortunately for the men none of their relatives thought they should drink.

"Only people who embrace the devil drink," Grace Brethren said.

"Did anybody ever tell you, you have great legs," Mr. Fist said to Grace Brethren.

"Mr. Fist," Nurse Steal scolded.

"She does," Jake Lost said.

"Heathens," Grace Brethren huffed.

Rose Merrywood winked at Mr. Fist. Mr. Fist blew her a kiss.

"Time for bingo," Hazel called. "Tonight we will be giving away pencils and writing paper, and we will have a dollar jackpot for the last game."

"Gambling," Grace Brethren snorted, although she sat through the bingo games to pray for the sinners.

Martha Dearheart pushed Rose Merrywood toward the

dayroom.

Nurse Steal did not normally stay for bingo, but Nurse Sly, the night nurse, was running late. Nurse Steal worked on paperwork at the nurses' station while Hazel got everybody ready for the night's game. Bertha Shields and Randolph were sitting next to Harold. Grace Brethren, Rose Merrywood, and Martha Dearheart had been joined by Wilma Happy, Betty Frost, and Gloria Sane. All of the women were wheelchair bound and reminded Nurse Steal of white-haired elves. They had each been a farmer's wife and had many things in common.

"If I win I don't have anyone to write to," Mr. Fist told Robert Begone, Jake Lost, and Paul Mouse. Jake Lost did not have his hearing aid in his ear, so he could not hear.

"All right, everybody has two bingo cards except Grace Brethren," Hazel said into a microphone.

"Randolph doesn't," Bertha Shields said.

Hazel gave Randolph two bingo cards.

"That's cheating," Robert Begone said.

"Who cares," Mr. Fist said. "The teddy bear can't count."

"Put your hearing aid in," Mr. Fist told Jake Lost.

"What?" Jake Lost said.

Nurse Steal observed the residents. "Halfway between heaven and earth," she thought trying to not feel sad.

"B-1," Hazel called.

"Oh, I have that one," Rose Merrywood said happily.

"G-10."

"Oh, I have that one also," Rose Merrywood said.

Grace Brethren prayed for the sinners around her.

A few minutes later Rose Merrywood hollered, "Bingo! Bingo!"

Hazel confirmed it was a good bingo. Rose Merrywood beamed as she received a new pencil and a small yellow notepad with white flowers on the paper. "It is so pretty," Rose Merrywood said.

Grace Brethren tried not to look at the paper, but she could not help herself. "It is pretty," she commented, then felt guilty.

"How come a woman always wins," George Early

grumbled. "I only had one number to go."

"It's a conspiracy," Henry Right said.

"You guys shut up so we can play another game," Jake Lost yelled, having finally adjusted his hearing aid.

"Shut up! Shut up!" Harold piped.

Randolph won the second game. "I knew that teddy bear could count," Robert Begone, highly perturbed, said to Mr. Fist.

Bertha Shields held the paper and pencil in front of Randolph.

"Randolph likes," Harold said.

Mr. Fist won the third game and the dollar. "If we could keep this up we could buy our own *Playboy*," Mr. Fist told his buddies.

"What," Jake Lost yelled, fiddling with his hearing aid again.

"*Playboy*," Robert Begone yelled.

"Tits," Harold called out.

"Dear Jesus," Grace Brethren muttered.

"Time for bed," Nurse Steal announced.

"Randolph is not tired," Bertha Shields protested.

"If Randolph is not well, he needs more rest," Hazel told Bertha Shields.

The residents made their way to their rooms while Hazel went to the medication room and put multi-colored pills into little paper cups for the nightly medications. "We have all lost our dreams," she said sadly, looking at the pills.

Rose Merrywood was in bed, the paper and pencil she had won was on the nightstand where she could see it. She did not know what the three pills were she had taken. She did know they helped her sleep and also made her feel less alone.

Martha Dearheart hung her dress in the closet and put on a long white cotton nightgown and went to bed. Gazing at the ceiling, she tried to formulate in her mind a plan on how to organize the residents to demand a few changes. There had to be more to life than being fed and playing games until death took one away. "This is more like a prison," she stated flatly and shut her eyes. "And we have done nothing wrong but grow old."

Grace Brethren was propped up in bed with a reading light

shining behind her. She held a worn and tattered Bible and stared out her window into the darkness. She could see the black outline of a tree and a few stars. "Dear God," she prayed. "Why must we all suffer so? Why do you fill my days with questions? Bless all the creatures of the earth."

Bertha Shields rested with only her head sticking out from underneath the covers. Randolph was on top of the covers. "If you are good, tomorrow Papa will take us for a ride," she said to the teddy bear. "We will ride out to the country and get to breathe some fresh air. You will like that. It will make you feel better."

The teddy bear seemed to smile. "I love you," Bertha Shields said.

"I love you too," Randolph said in Bertha Shields' mind.

Mr. Fist was in bed covered by a light blanket, but he was fully dressed. "One night I will break out of this joint," he pledged.

Jake Lost, deeply medicated, snored - his hearing aid ringing in his ears.

Robert Begone was completely perplexed. He could not figure out for the life of him who had stolen his shoes and then brought them back and put them under his bed. Whoever it was, he wished they would steal them and keep them. What was a thief if they did not keep what they stole?

Paul Mouse was in bed trying not to think about how lonely he was.

Henry Right was still angry that Randolph had won a bingo game and swore he would never play again as long as Randolph got to play.

Harold, wearing his pajamas covered with small red hearts, knelt down at the foot of his bed. Clasping his hands together, he prayed. "God bless all the people, and the children, and the birds, and Nurse Steal."

Nurse Steal was outside Harold's room. A single tear slid down her cheek and she wiped it off with the back of her hand. After Harold got into bed, she went in and pulled the covers up around his neck and kissed Harold on the forehead.

"Good boy," he said sleepily.

"Yes," Nurse Steal said. "You are a very good little boy."

Harold smiled and shut his eyes.

Nurse Sly was at the nurses' station. Nurse Sly was in her thirties and had moved to the area from St. Louis when her husband got a new job. They did not have any children, neither of them wanting to bring children into the modern world. She was short, with a medium build, and had long blond hair. Nurse Steal said goodnight pleasantly although she did not really like Nurse Sly. Nurse Sly never seemed to smile, and although she did her job well, she did it with remoteness and seemingly uncaring manner. But, at times, Nurse Steal wondered if it was Nurse Sly's way of hiding her sadness for the people. Either way most of the residents did not really like Nurse Sly either which in its own way was sad.

The buzzer sounded behind Nurse Steal. For a few minutes she stood by the door of her ten year old Ford breathing deeply the fresh air which was free from the smell of polish and disinfectant and medications. Backing out she looked at the darkened windows of Rest View and saw Mr. Fist's light come on. "You will never escape Mr. Fist," she said sadly. "Your days of freedom are gone forever."

Feeling tired she drove to her small apartment and another night with only her longing for company.

Chapter Three

Before sunrise, Martha Dearheart was fully awake. She did not get out of bed but gazed through a crack in the curtains into the dark. Martha Dearheart enjoyed this part of the day. It was as though the real world did not exist. For a few moments she was able to live in the shadow of her fantasies. She was not in Rest View. She was in another world where there were real dreams and hopes and plans for the future.

The horizon turned a deep shade of gray. She wondered if there was an old lady on the other side of the earth who was watching the sunset. If there was Martha Dearheart wished she could change places with the other woman and go back to sleep.

She heard a few birds begin to chirp tentatively and the screech of two cats as their wanderings crossed paths.

Martha Dearheart got out of bed and opened the curtains as far as they would go just as the sun cleared the trees. "If only you could heal," she said quietly.

Thirty minutes later Martha Dearheart was dressed and ready for the day. The majority of the residents were still sleeping or beginning to wake up. Martha Dearheart wished she could take a walk and feel the dew on her bare feet. She wished she could touch the trees and listen to the wind rustle through the branches. Beginning to drift away on a sea of wishes Martha Dearheart inhaled deeply. "Wishing never did anybody any good," she scolded herself. "Only action makes change."

Martha Dearheart headed to Rose Merrywood's room and entered the room apprehensively. "I'm still alive," Rose Merrywood said. "If I can call it that."

Martha Dearheart brought the wheelchair over to the edge of the bed and helped Rose get into the chair. Rose Merrywood would not allow Martha Dearheart to help her dress. She would only allow the nurses to help her. "What are friends for?" Martha Dearheart protested once.

"To help get one through life, not to get dressed," Rose Merrywood informed her firmly.

"I have something I want to tell you but I don't want you to think I am crazy," Rose Merrywood said sheepishly.

"We are all crazy in here," Martha Dearheart replied.

"Harold waits until he thinks we are all asleep and then he really does fly," Rose Merrywood said.

"Good for him," Martha Dearheart replied, not the least bit taken back. "At least he is doing something besides turning into a vegetable like the rest of us."

"Aren't we the testy one this morning?" Rose Merrywood said, adding, "I wish we could all fly."

"I have made up my mind. Today I am going to try to do something about this place," Martha Dearheart declared. "I am going to start an action committee and demand a few changes at Rest View."

"You sound as if we are all in jail," Rose Merrywood said.

"Aren't we?" Martha Dearheart declared, walking stiffly away.

Rose Merrywood wheeled herself over to the sink and ran water on a wash cloth. There are a few things that could be changed around here she thought, but she did not know if she had the nerve to join an action committee.

Mr. Fist got out of bed. Since he was fully dressed, he only had to slip on his shoes. He was angry with himself. He had stayed awake as long as he could, waiting for Nurse Sly to either fall asleep or go on her rounds, but he had dozed off and maybe missed his chance to escape.

Robert Begone came into the room wearing only one shoe. "You're still here?" he asked in surprise.

Mr. Fist gave him a dirty look. "Fell asleep," he grumbled.

"You wouldn't have made it anyway," Robert Begone said. "If we ever expect to break out of this joint we need a get away car waiting outside."

Mr. Fist looked at Robert Begone with newfound admiration. "My God," he exclaimed. "You're absolutely right, we need an outside man with a car."

Robert Begone looked at his feet. "Lord," he said. "Somebody already stole one of my shoes and the day has just begun."

Mr. Fist took Robert Begone by the elbow and they shuffled toward the dining area. "You know anybody who has a car?" he asked excitedly.

Jake Lost and Paul Mouse were already in the dining room when Mr. Fist and Robert Begone got there. Mr. Fist whispered to the two men. "I know how we can blow this joint."

"How?" Paul Mouse whispered back

"Blow what joint?" Jake Lost bellowed. "Speak up."

"Turn your hearing aid up," Mr. Fist hollered.

"What?" Jake Lost yelled.

"Forget it, I'll tell you later," Mr. Fist said, shaking his head.

Paul Mouse pulled Jake's hearing aid out of his ear and turned it up.

"Did you take my shoe?" Robert Begone asked Paul Mouse.

"I think Grace Brethren took it," Paul Mouse replied mischievously.

Robert Begone looked over at Grace Brethren disappointedly. "I thought she was such a religious person. Goes to show you can never tell about people," he said loudly to Jake Lost.

"I can hear you, you don't have to talk so loud," Jake Lost said.

Paul Mouse leaned over close to Mr. Fist. "Now tell me how

we can blow this joint," he whispered.

"We need a guy on the outside with a car," Mr. Fist whispered back.

Paul Mouse thought for a moment before saying, "It might be easier to dig a tunnel. The guy with the car might be a rat."

"That's a good idea also," Mr. Fist agreed.

Grace Brethren did not pay any attention to anyone in the dining room. In the morning she tried to block out the world and only keep in her mind the thought of God and her savior Jesus Christ. It was her hair shirt part of the day as Martha Dearheart called it.

One day, sitting in the dayroom, Martha Dearheart told Grace Brethren. "If you could you would wear a hair shirt."

"What is a hair shirt?" Grace Brethren asked.

"During the Middle Ages deeply religious people wore wool shirts under their real shirts because they were uncomfortable and they hurt and itched. They believed the pain was an act of penance for their sins."

Grace Brethren, her eyes blazing with religious fervor said, "I bet I can order one from Amazon."

Martha Dearheart wheeled Rose Merrywood next to Grace Brethren and sat next to Rose. "Rose, would you pray with me?" Grace Brethren asked.

Rose Merrywood bowed her head. "Bless all of us sinners," Grace Brethren's voice rang out. "Bless all of us who walk in the darkness and search for the light. Let your divine will flood us with your love and wisdom and let Satan be driven from our lives. Thank you for one more day to see your miracle and one more day to save our souls from the eternal darkness that awaits the non-believer. Amen."

"Amen," Rose Merrywood repeated.

"Hard to believe someone could pray after stealing one of my shoes," Robert Begone said.

"She's probably a Catholic," Paul Mouse said.

Wilma Happy, Betty Frost, and Gloria Sane wheeled into the dining room and clustered around Rose Merrywood, Grace Brethren, and Martha Dearheart. "Grace has saved our souls for the day," Martha Dearheart informed them.

"There are not enough prayers to save your soul," Grace Brethren retorted.

"I wonder what is for breakfast," Wilma Happy said.

"I know there will be prunes," Betty Frost scowled.

"I'm sick of prunes," Gloria Sane said.

"I'm so old I'm tired of eating," Rose Merrywood said.

Henry Right wheeled in and stopped next to George Early. He smiled at Wilma Happy, who blushed.

Martha Dearheart saw Wilma Happy blush and had a wicked thought, but then dismissed it. "No," she said to herself. "It couldn't be."

But, looking once more at Wilma Happy's face, she wondered. She remembered a movie she saw years earlier where a man made love to a woman in a wheelchair. Martha Dearheart laughed a delicious laugh.

"Impure thoughts are as bad as impure deeds," Grace Brethren said.

"Oh, toot," Wilma Happy said and winked at Martha Dearheart.

Harold finished tying his tennis shoes. "Good boy," he said, heading for the dining room and peering into all the rooms as he went. When he entered the dining room, he stuck his arms out and began to flap them like a bird. "I fly, I fly," he called.

"Look everybody, Harold is flying," Jake Lost announced.

Harold started skipping around the dining room, flapping his arms and yelling happily, "Fly, fly, fly."

Rose Merrywood started to flap her arms. Wilma Happy started flapping her arms. Betty Frost and Gloria Sane started to flap their arms. Soon everybody was flapping their arms except Grace Brethren.

Nurse Sly, returning from the medication room, seeing the residents flapping their arms was outraged. "Harold!" Her voice cut through the air like a dagger. "You sit down right this minute!"

Harold stopped in his tracks as though he was a bird felled by a blast from a hunter's shotgun. The room became deathly silent as all eyes turned toward Nurse Sly. "You sit down!" Nurse Sly ordered Harold once again.

Harold put his thumb in his mouth and cowered like a frightened puppy.

"You people act your age," Nurse Sly scolded.

Martha Dearheart became outraged. "It is none of your business how we act. As long as nobody is getting hurt, we can do what we want. Even fly," she said.

Nurse Sly's face turned a vivid red. "You can't talk to me like that," she retorted.

"You work for us," Martha Dearheart said. "Don't you ever forget it."

"I am going to report you to Mr. Dry," Nurse Sly threatened.

"I hope you do," Martha Dearheart said defiantly.

Mr. Fist stood. "You tell them," he agreed.

"Damn right," Robert Begone said.

"Damn right," George Early said.

Nurse Sly stomped out of the dining room. Martha Dearheart did not feel happy over the confrontation. She had a momentary urge to go after Nurse Sly and apologize, but she had done nothing wrong.

Grace Brethren smiled at Harold the way a mother smiles at her son who has been chastised unfairly by his father.

Rose Merrywood wheeled over to Harold and put her hand on his shoulder. "Don't worry," she said. "You fly anytime you want."

"Harold not bad boy," Harold said, taking his thumb out of his mouth.

"No, you are not a bad boy," Rose Merrywood said.

"Where is Bertha Shields?" Betty Frost asked.

"She told me Randolph took a turn for the worst and she does not want to get him out of bed," Wilma Happy said.

"Dear God," Grace Brethren said.

"Randolph is always sick," Robert Begone said.

"Must be in his gene pool," Jake Lost said.

Harold went over to Mr. Fist. "You teach me and the boys

how to fly and we can escape this place," Mr. Fist said.

"I teach," Harold said seriously.

"Hear that men," Mr. Fist said to Robert Begone, Jake Lost and Paul Mouse. "Harold will teach us how to fly and we can get out of this death trap."

"I'll be damned," Paul Mouse said. "That beats the hell out of digging a tunnel or getting a car."

"I'll be damned," Harold laughed.

Mr. Fist contemplated the idea. It really did not seem all that unreasonable.

"I wish Grace Brethren would give me my shoe back," Robert Begone said.

An aide stopped by Mr. Fist and held out a paper cup with three pills in it and a glass of orange juice. Mr. Fist popped the pills in his mouth and drank the juice in two gulps.

"You don't even know what you are taking," Paul Mouse said.

"I'm taking Procardia for my heart, Furosemide for my blood pressure and fluid retention, Coumadin to thin my blood, and at night Voltaren for my arthritis," Mr. Fist stated, annoyed that anyone would dare challenge his intelligence.

Paul Mouse took his cup from the aide and swallowed his pills. "What are you taking, smart guy?" Mr. Fist asked.

Paul Mouse gave Mr. Fist a dirty look and did not answer.

The aide gave Harold a glass with one pill in it. Harold put the pill in his mouth, took the juice and drank. When the aide walked away, Harold spit the pill out of his mouth and put it in his pocket. "No fly," he said seriously to Robert Begone who had seen him spit out the pill.

"Saltpeter," Robert Begone said.

After all the medications were distributed, another aide began passing out breakfast. There was oatmeal, peaches, dried prunes, whole-wheat toast and jelly, and coffee or tea.

George Early and Henry Right looked around the room to make sure no one was watching and put the prunes in their pockets. They smiled at each other - sure they now had enough fruit to make a batch of home brew.

Nurse Sly was relieved by Nurse Steal at the nurses' station. "Harold riled them all up again with his flying antics," Nurse Sly complained. "The poor man really thinks he can fly. Can you imagine?"

"No, I can only wish," Nurse Steal said.

"I overreacted," Nurse Sly said. "I hollered at Harold and had a few words with Martha Dearheart. I don't know why I get so short sometimes?"

"It's a difficult job," Nurse Steal said.

"I told Martha I was going to report her to Mr. Dry," Nurse Sly said.

"Are you?"

"No. Merely thinking about my statement makes me feel like an idiot. It seems at times I treat the people like they are children and not adults."

"I don't think I am a child or an adult," Nurse Steal said. "Most of the time I don't know what I am."

"Me either," Nurse Sly said as she left.

Nurse Steal announced, "Good morning, everyone," as she entered the dining room.

"Good morning," the residents replied in unison. Harold waved and grinned, not bothering to wipe off the oatmeal that dripped from his chin. Nurse Steal, hearing the good mornings and seeing the residence smiles felt warm and needed.

"Did you bring us a *Playboy*?" Mr. Fist asked hopefully.

"No, not today," Nurse Steal replied with a shake of her head.

When breakfast was over Martha Dearheart announced in a strong voice to the residents, "All people interested in forming an action committee to address necessary changes to Rest should meet me in the dayroom."

"Oh, this is exciting," Rose Merrywood said.

"The work of the devil," Grace Brethren said.

"This could be fun," Mr. Fist told his friends.

Harold timidly approached Nurse Steal. "Harold not bad boy," he said, his head falling to one side.

Nurse Steal ruffled his hair. "Nurse Sly was tired, she didn't mean anything," she told him.

"Harold teach Nurse Steal fly," Harold said seriously.

"Oh, Harold, I'm too big and fat to fly. I couldn't get this body off of the ground."

Harold stuck his thumb in his mouth and seemed to ponder the problem for a moment. Taking his thumb out of his mouth, he said. "No, big birds fly too. I teach."

"No Harold," Nurse Steal said, "Some people don't have the will to even try to fly anymore."

Harold watched Nurse Steal walk away and he headed for the dayroom. "Nurse Steal fly if Harold fly," he said.

An aide, overhearing him, shook his head in disbelief. "Poor simple bastard," he muttered.

In the dayroom Martha Dearheart was standing in front of the TV set. Rose Merrywood, Wilma Happy, Betty Frost, and Gloria Sane were directly in front of her. Grace Brethren was on the sofa. Mr. Fist, Robert Begone, Jake Lost and Paul Mouse were at a table. Nurse Steal was at the nurses' station filling out the morning report. Mr. Dry, having been informed by an aide the residents were trying to form an action committee, was in the hall out of view of the residents, but positioned so he could hear all that would go on. Mr. Dry had great respect for the residents of the home, but he also knew his duty was to his employer. A duty he staunchly followed although many times his heart was not in his decisions.

Martha Dearheart cleared her throat, but as she started to speak Harold walked over. "Randolph not here," he said.

"Randolph is sick," Rose Merrywood said.

"Harold go see," Harold said and headed for Bertha Shields' room.

"Don't forget you are going to teach us how to fly," Mr. Fist called to Harold.

"Me teach," Harold answered over his shoulder.

"Do you want to learn how to fly or be in this meeting?" Martha Dearheart asked Mr. Fist.

"Both," Mr. Fist replied truthfully.

Martha Dearheart sighed, took a deep breath and said, "I do

not want anybody to have any misconstrued ideas in their head about why I want this meeting. It is not like we are being held in a concentration camp. Nor is it the fact we are mistreated or not taken care of.

My complaints, and yours I am sure, have only to do with ways in which we can improve our situation."

"Well spoken," Rose Merrywood commented proudly.

"We should have opened the meeting with a prayer," Grace Brethren said.

"Who is she to talk? She stole my shoe," Robert Begone said.

The people gasped.

"She didn't steal your shoe. I was only kidding," Paul Mouse said.

"Then who stole it?" Robert Begone asked, looking confused.

"Shut up and let Martha talk," Mr. Fist ordered. "Your shoe is by your bed."

Martha Dearheart continued. "I am sure most people never think about living in a rest home until they are in one. But here we are. And if we can make changes it will only help those who follow us."

Wilma Happy started to cry. "I don't want to be here. I want to be home," she sobbed.

Betty Frost put her arm around Wilma Happy's shoulder. "Now, now," she said. "Nobody wants to be here."

"Why is my daughter so cruel?" Wilma Happy implored.

"Oh, Wilma, your daughter does not mean to be cruel. Surely you know that. There is no way she could take care of you at her home," Rose Merrywood said.

"If they loved me they would let me live at home," Wilma Happy sobbed.

"You poor thing," Grace Brethren said. "Of course they love you."

"It's not their fault," Mr. Fist soothed. "Everything is so expensive now nobody can stay home and take care of their loved ones."

Wilma Happy stopped crying. "I feel so useless and unwanted."

"We all love you," Jake Lost said.

"When my grandfather was in his nineties," Gloria Sane said, "he could no longer walk and very seldom spoke. My mother would push him out into the front yard and scatter birdseed around him. He would sit and watch the birds all day. My mother was letting him know he was still a part of life, still something that was needed. They make us old," she sighed. "They stick us in these homes and then forget about us as if we are not alive."

"We are born to suffer," Grace Brethren said. "Life is but tears and pain."

"It doesn't have to be," Martha Dearheart said sternly. "Somehow people have forgotten life is love and hope and not fear and control."

"We have to stand up for our rights as human beings," George Early said.

"If we don't, no one else will do it for us," Henry Right said.

"I think we should spend today thinking about things that can be changed around here and have another meeting tomorrow," Paul Mouse said.

"What a wonderful idea," Martha Dearheart said. "Tomorrow after breakfast we will meet again."

Martha Dearheart watched the people shuffle, wheel, and clink their way back to their rooms. She felt empty. Lunch was only a few hours away and then the ladies would meet and it would be another day - another day gone to nowhere.

As Martha Dearheart went by the nurses' station, Nurse Steal said, "I hope all goes well with your meetings."

"Help us," Martha Dearheart implored.

"I need this job," Nurse Steal replied sadly. "I can't take sides."

"We need our pride and dignity," Martha Dearheart answered.

Bertha Shields, fully dressed, lay on top of the covers. Randolph was wrapped tightly in a light blanket. Harold was by the bed.

"Randolph like fly," Harold said.

"Randolph is too sick," Bertha Shields said. "I don't know if he is going to get better or not. It might be better if he just died."

"No die," Harold said. "Harold loves Randolph."

Bertha Shields adjusted the blanket under Randolph's chin. "Did you hear that, Randolph?" she said softly. "Harold loves you and I love you. Now why don't you get better?"

The teddy bear's eyes were fixed on the ceiling. "He finally fell asleep," Bertha Shields said.

Harold tip-toed toward the door.

"Thank you for coming to see how Randolph is doing," Bertha Shields said.

"Harold good boy," Harold whispered.

George Early put some prunes and raisins in the quart jar, along with sugar and a half slice of bread. He then filled the jar with water and screwed the lid on tightly. He hid the jar in his closet with three others, feeling like he had just pulled off the biggest bank job in the history of the world.

Mr. Dry did not miss a word during the meeting of the residents. Now he was deeply concerned. He knew small inconsequential happenings could lead to earth shattering movements. He did not want to see this happen at Rest View. Rubbing his balding head he took a deep breath. He felt older than his fifty years, and at five feet six inches and slightly overweight he felt tired, but he knew the tiredness came more from his responsibilities than his age or weight. He saw his reflection in a small framed mirror on the wall. His face was soft and his eyes were dull. He adjusted his tie and glanced at the photograph of his wife and three children on his desk, wondering what his children would do with him when he was old. "I never want to be in a rest home," he said, but he could think of no other option.

Mr. Dry went to the nurses' station. Nurse Steal was just finishing her morning report and was going over the new medication chart. "I would like to talk to you in my office," Mr.

Dry informed her.

Nurse Steal hated it when she had to go to Mr. Dry's office. She always felt like a small girl who was about to be chastised by her father. Mr. Dry was always distant and did not really interact with the residents, which to Nurse Steal should have been the biggest aspect of his job. She also thought he dressed too formally for the job. He always wore a heavily starched shirt with a tie. To Nurse Steal formal attire made her feel that Mr. Dry felt he was superior to the residents and not their biggest advocate, but she was not brave enough to tell him.

"Sit down," Mr. Dry said, pointing at a chair in front of his desk.

Nurse Steal looked calmly at Mr. Dry. She did not like the man, but she did not dislike him either. They were on two different sides of the fence but they both needed each other.

"The residents have me worried," Mr. Dry said.

"I don't think there is anything to worry about," Nurse Steal said.

"I hope not, but I want you to keep me informed on anything you hear. If they plan anything, we must be one step in front of them."

Nurse Steal hated the word 'we.' 'We' had nothing to do with it. Her job was to give medications and help any way she could. When it came to administration she had no responsibility whatsoever. Policy was for the board.

Nurse Steal was relieved leaving Mr. Dry's office and glanced at her watch. It was time for her to check on the bedridden residents.

******

Sunlight filled the room, but was absorbed by the dull gray oxygen tank standing by the bed. An ancient man lay on the bed with an oxygen mask strapped to his face. The only way Nurse Steal could tell he was breathing was by the slight movement of his emaciated chest. By all rights she knew the man should be in the hospital, but what with the enormous cost of hospitalization, it was easier for the family to keep him at Rest View. Nurse Steal checked the gauges on the tank, picked up the man's thin arm to check his pulse, and set his arm carefully back down by his side. She pulled the light cotton blanket off of him and checked his diaper. He was not soiled so she re-covered the frail body. She stepped over to the window and felt like she was in a fish bowl. Here, in this room, was the end of life, and just on the other side of the glass was a world so far removed the man was cursed to never enter it again. "Dear Lord, how can you make some of us live so long?" she questioned. But she thought of the Digitalis, and the Lasix, and the Coumadin, and Motrin, flowing through the frail body and she knew her question was not altogether proper. She looked once more at the man, and left the room with a heavy heart. After checking on four other bedridden patients, she started for the dining room. It was almost time for lunch. "I hope they aren't serving peas," she said with a wry smile.

Mr. Dry said hello to Rose Merrywood, smiled to Grace Brethren, and nodded at Mr. Fist and his crew of troublemakers. When Martha Dearheart came by he stopped her. "I would like to speak with you for a few minutes," he said.

"Why certainly, Mr. Dry," Martha Dearheart replied, thinking to herself that Mr. Dry was really the Big Bad Wolf trying to figure out a way to eat Little Red Riding Hood.

Mr. Dry held out the chair for Martha Dearheart to sit before sitting at his desk. He searched Martha Dearheart's face, but could not detect even a trace of fear or insecurity in her piercing eyes. "Mrs. Dearheart," he began. "It has come to my attention you have started an action group to try and make changes at Rest View."

"Correct," Martha Dearheart replied crisply.

Mr. Dry drummed his fingertips on the top of the desk. "I have nothing against what you are trying to do," he said. "But I do want you to know Rest View is a very large and powerful chain of rest homes and they would be very slow to change."

"I love a challenge," Martha Dearheart said calmly.

"I want you to know we will work with you as much as we can," Mr. Dry said.

"I am sure you will. But right now I am hungry and lunch

will soon be served."

"You must understand," Mr. Dry said. "The big insurance companies control everything. I would love to see you have more freedom but I don't know if it is possible."

"We want dignity. Is it too much to ask?" Martha Dearheart stated defiantly as she left.

"I would like dignity myself," Mr. Dry said to himself. "At times I feel like I am only a pawn and that I have never fought hard enough for what I believe in."

Martha Dearheart was excited for the first time in years. "I love a good fight," Martha Dearheart said to Rose Merrywood.

"I have always been a coward," Rose Merrywood said. "But now that I am so old, I suppose there is nothing really to be afraid of."

"Nothing but ourselves," Martha Dearheart said.

Everybody was quiet and subdued during lunch. It seemed like all the residents were confused - wanting to voice their complaints, but they could not rid themselves of the idea that in all truth they were prisoners, and prisoners do not have any rights that one can speak of.

After lunch Martha Dearheart did not take a nap, but sat by the window with her jewelry box in her lap and gazed fondly at the garnet and pearl pins. Taking one last look at the pins, she set the box on top of her dresser, and for a moment she felt she should stop her crusade before it even started. Maybe change was not in order? Maybe if everyone kept the same routine they would be happier - happy to sit and vegetate and die quietly like they were supposed to. Martha Dearheart shut her eyes, but immediately reopened them and said defiantly, "Well, if they do, they can go to hell."

******

Grace Brethren, Rose Merrywood, Wilma Happy, Betty Frost, Gloria Sane and Randolph and Bertha Shields were already at the table when Martha Dearheart entered the dayroom. George Early and Henry Right were arguing loudly over a checker move, while Mr. Fist and his men had Harold surrounded in a corner looking like detectives who had their man collared.

"I see Randolph is feeling better," Martha Dearheart said.

Bertha Shields patted the head of the teddy bear. "I think he finally knows we all love him," she said.

Wilma Happy reached over and touched the nose of Randolph. "You silly dear," she said. "You should have known we all love you."

"Harold convinced him," Bertha Shields said. "Harold even wants to teach him how to fly."

Grace Brethren was about to say something when Martha Dearheart said, "Don't you say a word Grace."

Grace Brethren gave her a dirty look.

"I think Harold should give all of us flying lessons," Betty Frost said. "It would be better exercises than the nurses have us do and at least it would be fun."

"It would make Harold feel good," Rose Merrywood said.

"That should be one of our demands, we get to take flying lessons," Gloria Sane said.

Grace Brethren could no longer control herself. "Somebody should tell Harold people cannot fly and anyone who thinks they can is an idiot."

The other ladies did not bother to answer Grace Brethren. Grace Brethren, waiting for a retort, was put back by the silence. Nurse Steal stopped by the table. "I want you all to know that I feel Mr. Dry will do his best to help you. But you cannot push him too far. There is only so much he can do."

"Thank you for your advice," Martha Dearheart said. "But I am confident we can manage our affairs in a democratic way and I can assure you our demands will be rational."

"I am on your side," Nurse Steal said and started to leave, but the word 'demand' made her feel uneasy and she turned back to Martha Dearheart. "I think you should call your demands recommendations," she said. "It might get you further."

"You are right," Martha Dearheart said, "thank you."

Nurse Steal smiled.

Martha Dearheart could see fear on the ladies faces. She

knew they looked to her for their strength. It was imperative she not show any weakness, even if in her heart she too felt there might not be any hope.

Mr. Fist was excited. Robert Begone had forgotten he only had one shoe on. Jake Lost, for once with his hearing aid set correctly, was so deep in thought he looked like he had fallen asleep with his eyes open. Paul Mouse was scratching every part of his body like he had fleas. "Now listen, Harold," Mr. Fist said. "I am old enough to know a man can do anything he sets his mind to. There is nothing that is impossible. One only has to believe and work hard and every dream can come true. Our dream is to break out of this place. We don't want to die in here, cut off from the world. You teach us how to fly and we'll bust out of this joint."

"Who is old?" Jake Lost called out. "You are only as old as you feel."

"Yes, well, I feel like crap," Mr. Fist said.

"Me to," Robert Begone agreed.

"If you tell me you feel like a young man, you're a lying dog," Paul Mouse sneered.

"If Harold could teach us how to fly we would still only be able to fly as fast as old birds anyway," Jake Lost said.

"He's right," Mr. Fist said dejectedly. "What good would it be to fly if we could only fly a few feet and then have to stop and rest?"

"My shoe is gone again," Robert Begone said.

"You really know how to kill a party, Jake," Paul Mouse said.

"No, I teach fly," Harold beseeched the men.

Mr. Fist patted Harold on the shoulder. "Oh Harold," he said. "I guess we all have to learn to control our dreams. We just have to accept what life has dealt us and live with it."

Mr. Fist headed dejectedly toward his room.

Rose Merrywood watched Mr. Fist and thought to herself, you poor man, you poor, poor old man.

With Mr. Fist gone, the other men sat silently for a few moments before Jake Lost said, "It would be easier to find somebody with a get away car."

Robert Begone and Paul Mouse did not reply but got up and left. Jake Lost fiddled with his hearing aid. "Life is better when you can't hear," he said, heading to his room.

Harold, left alone, put his thumb in his mouth and let his head fall so his chin was almost touching his chest. "I fly," he whispered. "I fly like bird, everybody fly. Harold good boy."

The ladies were busy watching two young men planting marigolds in the freshly dug flowerbed outside the window.

"I would like to have a small flower garden," Grace Brethren said, surprising everyone. Nobody thought Grace would like to do anything in life besides pray.

"Bring that up in the meeting tomorrow," Rose Merrywood said.

"I will do that," Grace Brethren said. "There is no reason we could not have a small garden or a plot of flowers of our own."

Bertha Shields wheeled her wheelchair away from the table. "I had better take Randolph back. He is doing so much better I would not want to see him get sick again."

"I will go back with you," Grace Brethren said. "I have a few more ideas I want to write down."

Wilma Happy, Betty Frost, and Gloria Sane also left.

Rose Merrywood watched as one of the men put a marigold in the ground and carefully patted the soil around it. "I wasn't kidding when I told you I really do believe Harold can fly," she said to Martha Dearheart.

"He can fly only in his mind. It is the only thing that keeps him alive," Martha Dearheart said.

Rose Merrywood glanced over at Harold. "I wonder what life is like when one really never knows what is going on in the world," she said.

"It is probably very lonely but it could also be a blessing," Martha Dearheart answered.

"I hope it is a blessing," Rose Merrywood said. "But I still think he can fly."

"I hope you are right," Martha Dearheart said. "For all the lonely people, I hope he can."

"I think all of mankind is lonely," Rose Merrywood said and started toward her room.

Martha Dearheart watched the men plant more flowers. She did not notice George Early and Henry Right both knock their checkers to the floor and wheel their chairs out of the day- room in a huff. Nor did she see Nurse Steal talking quietly to Harold. She could see herself soaring high above Rest View. She could feel the fresh air on her skin. Shutting her eyes she could imagine herself flying toward the sun. The sun was so bright she could see nothing else, only the flaming yellow orb that seemed to beckon her and pull her into its inferno. "I will cause change," she stated, reopening her eyes. "This place will never forget me."

Nurse Steal watched Martha Dearheart leave the dayroom and then she and Harold picked up the checkers. When they were done Nurse Steal hugged Harold. "Harold good boy," Harold said. "I teach fly, Randolph, Bertha, all people I teach fly."

Nurse Steal brushed his hair back from his forehead and smiled sadly.

******

Her shift over, Nurse Steal headed slowly toward her car, a thin veil of clouds covered the stars, but it was still a bright enough night she cast a faint shadow as she walked.

She stopped by her car, took a cigarette out of her purse, and lit it. She did not smoke often, but at the moment she felt like it and inhaled deeply. Supper had gone off without a hitch. The residents had eaten all their food, watched TV, and filed off to bed. Nurse Steal took another deep drag on the cigarette. Rest View lay in a dull glow, the hall lights slicing into the darkness like a knife. If I was old I would want to sleep in the dark she thought. Nurse Steal liked the dark. There was something about the dark that made her feel not so vulnerable to life - something about the dark that held her safe and secure from the daytime. After butting the cigarette on the ground she dug her keys out of her purse. But as she got into her car she could picture Martha Dearheart looking at her pearl and garnet pins. She could see

53

Rose Merrywood wishing she could walk. She could see Grace Brethren with her hair free from its severe bun and praying. She smiled thinking about Mr. Fist hoping this would be the night Nurse Sly would fall asleep and he could make his break. And she could see Harold standing by his window flapping his arms and dreaming he could fly.

Nurse Steal put the keys into the ignition and turned on the lights. As she was about to start the car a bird sang, "Fa, La, La." For some reason the song made her feel both happy and sad. She did not start the car but peered outside. She remembered a poem when she was a child about a night bird, but she could not remember the words, although they rested on the tip of her tongue. Once again the bird sang, "Fa, La, La." "Poor lonely little bird," she murmured.

Just then a small brown bird, with a splash of blue on its breast dipped and circled through the beam from the headlights and then flew around the car singing its three-note song. "Fa, La, La, Fa, La, La."

Nurse Steal stuck her head out of the window as the bird landed on the hood. The little bird's head was cocked to one side as he sang, "Fa, La, La, Fa, La, La." For some strange reason the bird reminded her of Harold.

"Fa, La, La," Nurse Steal sang back.

Headlights from another car swept over her. Nurse Steal waved at a police car as it circled the parking lot. The police officer waved back. When she looked back the bird was gone. What a nice bird, Nurse Steal thought.

Driving to her apartment Nurse Steal felt content and she hoped she would see the bird again

Harold's feet settled silently on the floor. He let his arms fall to his sides. Rose Merrywood's called to him. "Harold, are you back?"

Harold looked down the hall to see if Nurse Sly was there. She wasn't so he tip-toed to Rose Merrywood's room. "I fly," he whispered to her.

"I know," Rose Merrywood said. "But nobody will believe you or me."

"You believe. Why not others?" Harold asked.

"The world has made it hard to believe in anything," Rose Merrywood said.

"Sad," Harold said, putting his thumb in his mouth and tiptoeing back to his room.

Chapter Four

Martha Dearheart waited patiently for the people to get situated. Rose Merrywood, Wilma Happy, and Gloria Sane had their wheelchairs directly to her front. George Early and Henry Right were slightly off to the right of the three ladies. "How is the brew doing?" George Early asked Henry Right. Henry Right gave him a thumbs up.

Robert Begone, Jake Lost, Paul Mouse and Mr. Fist were behind Rose Merrywood. Bertha Shields, with Randolph on her lap, was slightly away from the group. Grace Brethren was by the window, sternly overlooking the gathering. The other residents did not wish to attend. Harold walked nervously back and forth behind the people. Nurse Steal was at the nurses' station. Two aides, spies for Mr. Dry, were trying to make themselves look busy in the west hall. Martha Dearheart cleared her throat and started to speak. "Wait," Jake Lost shouted. "I have to adjust my hearing aid."

Everyone gave Jake Lost a disgusted look.

"Lord," Robert Begone said, "this time somebody took both of my shoes."

Martha Dearheart started to speak but was cut off by Grace Brethren. "We need a prayer," she stated forcefully.

"A prayer won't hurt us," Rose Merrywood said.

"Dear Lord," Grace Brethren began. "We are gathered here today to try and find dignity, please....."

"Amen," Mr. Fist cut in.

"Amen," the others said piously.

"Amen," Grace Brethren said, knowing that at times even faith has to bow to the powers that be.

For a brief instant Martha Dearheart was afraid she was not up to the task, and it was all a stupid idea, but she saw the eyes of her friends waiting anxiously for her words. She took several deep breaths and began. "When I was a young girl I always looked forward to seeing my grandparents. They were everything to me. I never thought of them as being old, or thought that they were once young. They were to me entities in life that had always been just the way they were. In my grandfather's whiskered and wrinkled face was an understanding that seemed only to be for me. My grandmother's stories of her earlier life were tales that stretched my imagination further than any movie or TV has or ever will. Even now I can still see my grandparents when I was young. I can still feel the strength and fortitude they gave me. I can hear at times my grandfather's chuckles at small trivial things I felt were so earth shattering and important."

Martha Dearheart paused, remembering her grandfather's and grandmother's funerals. "I know now my grandparents lived as much on the love that I felt for them as I lived for theirs. I know that in old age, as in young, we were both parts of a unity that binds life and lives together. We are the beginning and the end, each of us, young and old, something to be cherished and held dear - something that should never be separated."

Bertha Shields pressed Randolph close to her chest. "But time has changed what was," Martha Dearheart continued. "As time always will. What has happened to old people like us is not our fault, life has just changed and I suppose we must face the change. But we must also make changes ourselves. Nobody else will do it for us."

Wilma Happy started crying. "I only want to die at home. Is that too much to ask?"

"No cry, no cry, please," Harold implored.

"We cannot die at home," Betty Frost said matter of factly. "You must realize that Wilma, modern life has taken that honor from us. Unless you are fortunate both a wife and husband have to work just to make ends meet."

Wilma Happy choked back her tears and took a hanky that Gloria Sane handed her. "I know," she tried to say without her voice cracking. "I guess I am not as strong as the rest of you."

"We love you, we love you," Harold said. "Please, no cry."

"We have to accept what is," Martha Dearheart said with more conviction in her voice than she felt in her heart. "We have to do what we can to bring dignity back into our lives. We can no longer be herded and guided like unthinking and uncaring beasts. If we are to be human beings we have to take charge of at least a portion of our lives."

"Damn right," Mr. Fist yelled, jumping up from his chair and shaking his fist in the air.

"Mr. Fist," Rose Merrywood scolded. "We do not need profanity."

"Thank you, Rose," Grace Brethren said.

"Damn right," Harold called out.

"Dear Jesus," Grace Brethren muttered.

"Does anybody have a handkerchief?" Bertha Shields asked. "Randolph has a runny nose."

Paul Mouse handed Bertha Shields a handkerchief.

Bertha Shields, after holding the handkerchief under the teddy bear's nose, held it out for Paul Mouse to take back.

"No, keep it. It's dirty now," Paul Mouse said.

"What are we to do?" Rose Merrywood asked Martha Dearheart. "We are so helpless."

"That is why I have called this meeting. We need changes around here. I am open to all suggestions," Martha Dearheart replied, holding up a pen and notepad for everybody to see. "I will write down all the suggestions and present them to Mr. Dry."

"Speaking for myself and my friends, we feel Rest View should get us a subscription to *Playboy*," Mr. Fist said.

"What we look at is nobody's business," Jake Lost said.

"It's our right," Robert Begone said. "They have no right to regulate what we read or look at."

"I take it you don't read the newspaper," George Early said. "All the politicians want to do anymore is tell people what they can and can't do."

Martha Dearheart wrote - Playboy, a constitutional right.

"Anyone else?" Martha Dearheart asked.

"I don't think we should have to have a nurse or aide with us if we want to go outside," Robert Begone said.

Martha Dearheart wrote - Make it easier for the men to escape.

Henry Right said. "I think it would help if the nurses and the aides dressed like normal people. With their uniforms I feel like I am either in the nut house or the hospital. If they dressed in normal clothes it would cheer this place up. This is supposed to be a home, a place to live out our last years. I don't know of anybody who wears a uniform at home."

Martha Dearheart wrote - Have employees look like people, not scientists.

Grace Brethren said. "I think we should have real plants in the dayroom, not these fake plastic ones. We should also be allowed to have a small flowerbed and garden outside that we can take care of. We have to be able to get out more. This place is like a sterile bubble, a bubble that keeps us from the real world."

"I can grow onions," George Early said.

"And tomatoes," Bertha Shields said.

"Flowers," Wilma Happy said.

Martha Dearheart wrote - Garden and flowers, real plants in the dayroom, get rid of plastic.

"Would we have to pray around the garden everyday?" Robert Begone asked.

"Only if you wanted to," Grace Brethren said.

"I want to go fishing," Mr. Fist said.

Martha Dearheart wrote - Mr. Fist, fishing.

"Even if we get changes around here it will not stop us from being old," Betty Frost said sadly. "We need something that will make us feel young."

"I know, I know," Rose Merrywood called happily. "We could have Harold give us flying lessons."

"I teach fly," Harold grinned, stretching his arms out and flapping them up and down.

"I'd take them," Mr. Fist said.

"Me too," Robert Begone said.

"I would too," Jake Lost said. "Even if I could only fly slow."

"We could call it Harold's Flying Aerobics Class and have it every day in the dayroom," Martha Dearheart said.

"Poor simple thing," Grace Brethren said to herself. But looking at Harold, she had a strange thought that maybe sin was something man had invented, and in truth, people were born into the light, and only slowly worked themselves into the darkness, but none-the-less "I would never stoop to such foolishness," she said.

"You might," Martha Dearheart said.

"I want bird," Harold called out, but he could not think of the last word, and with a desperate look on his face he formed his arms in a circle. "Bird, bird," he said again.

"Birdbath," Robert Begone said. "He thinks there should be a birdbath outside."

"Birdbath, birdbath," Harold hollered, jumping up and down with joy.

"We could put the bath by the window at the end of the east wing. Then we could all sit and watch the birds," Rose Merrywood said.

"Birdbath," Harold called out again and started to flap his arms wildly.

"Take it easy," Mr. Fist said to Harold. "We don't want you flying out of here before you have a chance to teach us all how to fly."

Grace Brethren, watching Harold, wished that just once in her life she could feel joy.

Martha Dearheart wrote - Birdbath, better than TV. "Is there anything else?" she asked.

"I want whiskey," George Early said.

"And beer," Mr. Fist said.

"Dancing women once a month," Robert Begone said.

Rose Merrywood laughed. Grace Brethren shook her head.

Martha Dearheart dutifully wrote - Beer, whiskey, women.

"Anything else?" she asked.

"I think the buzzer should be taken off the door," Rose Merrywood said. "We are not prisoners."

"It would make it easier to blow this joint," Mr. Fist whispered to Paul Begone.

Martha Dearheart wrote - No buzzer, this is not a submarine.

When nobody said anything else, Martha Dearheart said, "I want us to be able to close our doors all the way." She wrote - Close doors.

"It is almost lunchtime," Nurse Steal announced. "After lunch the children from the First Methodist Church will be here to sing a few songs for us. Everybody should attend."

"Do we have to?" Mr. Fist complained.

"You don't have to, but they think we all enjoy their singing, so it would be nice of you,"

Martha Dearheart replied.

"Fa, La, La," Harold sang in beautiful crystal clear notes.

Nurse Steal's head snapped up from her work and she stared at Harold in disbelief, the three note song burning in her mind. The three notes the little brown bird, with a splash of blue on its breast, was singing the night it flew around her car

"Are there anymore ideas?" Martha Dearheart asked.

No one said anything else.

"With nothing else on the agenda, I call this meeting to a close," Martha Dearheart announced.

The two aides who had been spying headed quickly to Mr. Dry's office.

******

Martha Dearheart opened her jewelry box and touched the pearl pin and then the garnet pin. She felt like she should wear both of them at all times. It was strange, but when she wore one she felt as though she was cheating the other one, although she did not want to feel a preference for one over the other. But, in all truth, she had a preference for the garnet pin her husband had given her.

Shutting the jewelry box, she looked out the window. Each passing day brought more shades of green to the grass and soon the trees would be in full foliage. She did not want to think about the winter to come but keep her mind on each day.

Mr. Fist examined the white squares of linoleum covering the floor. He wondered if he could steal a knife from the kitchen and peel up several of the squares so cleanly the janitor could not tell. Then with time he could pick through the concrete foundation and start digging a hole. It was only a few feet to the outside of his window - only a few feet to freedom. He did not care if he could get far away. He would just like to escape and die outdoors. Die away from his captors. Die in one last moment of freedom and glory.

He remembered reading a story about the early Eskimos and how when an Eskimo got old and was too much of a burden for the family to manage they would walk away from the igloo and sit on the ice to die. Mr. Fist wanted to run away from Rest View and sit with the trees and die. "I am a man," he called out, shaking his fist, "You have forgotten that."

Rose Merrywood was in the hall and could see into Harold's room. Harold was standing in front of his window and he was flapping his arms slowly. She could not hear what he was saying, but she knew he was talking to himself. "I only want to fly once," she said to herself. She smiled and stretched out her arms and flapped them several times up and down. "Oh, if I could only escape this wheelchair once more before I die."

Rose Merrywood stopped flapping her arms and wheeled into her room and stopped by the window. She saw two birds flying. "I can fly if Harold flies," she murmured as if in prayer.

Robert Begone was in his room staring in amazement at both of his shoes by the end of his bed. "I wonder who keeps doing this to me," he mused. "You would think if they really wanted my shoes they would not keep returning them." For an instant he felt sad, wondering if there was somebody in the home that did not have any shoes and occasionally borrowed his. He remembered when he was a child on a farm in Ohio and how he and his three brothers only had one pair of shoes each and how precious they were. Robert picked up his shoes. He put one shoe on and looking at his clock saw it was time for lunch. He headed for the dining room with only one shoe on. Paul Mouse was shuffling toward the dining room. Robert Begone caught up with him. "Somebody must have stolen one of your shoes again," Paul Mouse said.

"I'll be damned," Robert Begone said, shaking his head. "I had both of them just a few minutes ago. Whoever it is must be a really good thief."

Nurse Steal had not completely recovered from the confusion she felt when Harold sang Fa, La, La exactly like the bird by her car. She did feel happy the residents had mentioned they wanted to take flying lessons. The residents needed an exercise period that was fun. She did not feel there was anything wrong with any of the recommendations the residents had brought up. She would just as soon wear clothes that were comfortable and colorful and not her uniform. She could see no reason for the men not to have a *Playboy*. Men were men, simple, dumb, and needing love, even if it was misdirected. Nurse Steal knew men and women were different and each had different roles in life. It was merely finding a happy middle ground. But, being a nurse, and being very practical, she knew love was not something that one wished for and it happened. She had longed for love for so many years now she knew how to deal with her loneliness and her longing. But maybe in her longing was the seed that made her such a good nurse, and maybe it was her loneliness that made her sympathetic. Maybe if she had a husband at home who made demands on her she would no longer feel the need or the desire to help others. Heading toward the dining room Nurse Steal passed Robert Begone and Paul Mouse. Robert Begone smiled at her. "If all the people who worked here were like you we would be very fortunate," he said to her.

For a moment Nurse Steal's veil of loneliness was lifted.

Nurse Steal was surprised to find Mr. Dry in the dining room. "I bet Mr. Dry is here because we are having peas," Rose Merrywood said to Martha Dearheart.

"I doubt it," Martha Dearheart said.

With Mr. Dry in the dining room, the residents felt as though he was the principle of a school and they were the students. After lunch was finished which consisted of baked fish, salad, an orange, and peas, which Martha Dearheart and Rose Merrywood gave to Harold, Mr. Dry raised his hand to let the residents know he had something to say. The room grew silent. Mr. Dry began. "I understand there are many things about having to live at Rest View that many of you do not agree with. I know Martha Dearheart has started a movement to try and remedy some of these things. And I want you all to know before we go on that I applaud your rights as Americans to proceed in any way you see fit, after all this is a democracy, but you should know that we, the members of the staff and myself, are only people and cannot be expected to be perfect. We are understaffed, and constantly being bombarded with new regulations and insurance guidelines that we have to live by."

Mr. Fist leaned over to Robert Begone. "If the cheap bastards would pay a livable wage they wouldn't be understaffed."

"Do you have a comment?" Mr. Dry asked Mr. Fist.

"No," Mr. Fist answered. "I was only telling Robert Begone what a pleasing voice you have."

Rose Merrywood giggled, but stopped immediately when Mr. Dry gave her a sharp look.

Mr. Dry went on. "You all must know that the policies here are not set solely by me."

"We want *Playboy*," Jake Lost yelled.

"We want whiskey," George Early yelled.

"We want to go fishing," Robert Begone yelled.

"Birds, birds, birds," Harold called and started skipping around the room and flapping his arms up and down.

"Fly away, Harold," Mr. Fist yelled.

Grace Brethren started praying out loud. "Dear God, in times of trouble I call to thee, lead me in the way of righteousness and make me invisible to mine enemies."

The room turned into mass confusion with everybody making demands and Harold skipping and flapping his arms faster and faster.

Martha Dearheart hollered, "Silence!"

Instantly the room grew quiet and Harold froze in his tracks. Martha Dearheart said to Mr. Dry. "I am sure that all of us gathered here are well aware of your position, Mr. Dry. And you can rest assured what we will ask for will not be things that we know cannot be changed or would cause any member of the staff any hardship or extra work. We only wish, in any way possible, to live our lives with as much dignity as we can. Is it too much to ask?"

"Believe me, I understand," Mr. Dry said. "I just don't want your expectations to be too high," and he left the room.

Mr. Fist called after him. "We also want a car parked outside with the keys in it."

With the excitement over, the residents headed back to their rooms for their afternoon nap. Nurse Steal said to Martha Dearheart, "If you have time I would like to talk to you."

"I have nothing but time, it may be limited, but it is time," Martha Dearheart said.

Martha Dearheart and Nurse Steal watched the janitor sweep hundreds of peas into a large rolling pile. "I want you to know I have changed my mind and I will help you in any way I can. What that would be, I don't know. But I will help."

"You will grow old," Martha Dearheart said. "Maybe what we try to do will help others."

"Maybe in time science will have a pill that stops us from getting old," Nurse Steal said.

"They might," Martha Dearheart replied, "but you would reach a point in your life you were mentally so tired you would want to die anyway. I don't think it's the body giving out so much that wears us down, it's the mind that has finally had enough."

"Maybe it is just the world," Nurse Steal sighed.

"Dear lady, to be a nurse you must always live in the world of grief and suffering and that has to make one old," Martha Dearheart said.

"There is love," Nurse Steal said. "Hidden in the cracks, dusty in forgotten corners, there is love."

Martha Dearheart smiled sadly and went to her room.

Nurse Steal stood by the window. The sky was the color of Harold's eyes and Nurse Steal imagined Harold's singing. Fa, La, La, Fa, La, La. Holding out her large and flabby arms she moved them up and down slowly. "Fa, La, La," she whispered and let her arms fall heavily to her sides. Dreamers only get crushed, she thought, heading for her rounds of the bedridden residents.

Martha Dearheart was trying to figure out the best way to proceed now that she had the resident's demands. There must be no mistakes when she submitted her letter, but she would take Nurse Steal's advice and call her demands recommendations. She had read somewhere that one must know the enemy to defeat them, and she realized she did not really know the enemy. She went over to her dresser and opened her jewelry box. A wave of disbelief and anguish swept over her such intensity she felt she might faint. The garnet and pearl pins were gone. A mournful cry tried to escape from her throat. She shut her eyes and sobbed, holding the cry inside. She could see the eyes of her husband, and the smile on her son's face when she had received both pins. "Who would do such a thing?" she pleaded.

With trembling hands she put the jewelry box in the top drawer of her dresser. "I will not say a word," she said out loud. "I will not let anybody know and maybe the thief will return the pins."

Martha Dearheart collapsed on the bed and pulled the blanket tight to her chin. But the blanket did not take away the cold.

In another room, a person stared at a garnet pin and a pearl pin that nestled in their palm like sleeping fairies - the person did not smile or feel elation over their treachery.

Chapter Five

Nurse Steal observed the bed confined woman. The woman's breathing came in slight raspy gurgles that seemed to emit from her throat and not her lungs. Her thin arms were no more than an inch around at the wrist, and her hair was so thin the dry skin of her scalp showed through like the crust on an apple pie. The room smelled of urine. Moving the lady as carefully as possible, Nurse Steal changed her diaper and the cloth sheet, which was over a rubber sheet. She wondered what went on in the woman's mind. Maybe she lived a life in her subconscious that was filled with more meaning than she had ever experienced when she knew reality. Maybe she had finally found the truth in life. Maybe the day to day existence of life was intended to be fulfilled by being oblivious to fear, or hope, or love, or hate - merely raspy gurgles of breath that possessed all true meaning.

Nurse Steal tenderly brushed the ladies thin straw like hair. She then trimmed the lady's fingernails and toenails. Before leaving, she patted the old lady's arm, "Live well in your dreams," she murmured as a prayer.

Going through the dayroom, Nurse Steal was surprised to see Harold sitting at the table the ladies normally occupied after their nap. She went over to him. Harold held up three fingers. "Two birds," he said happily.

Two sparrows were dusting themselves in the freshly planted flowerbed. "Yes, Harold, two birds," she said, not bothering to correct his number of fingers.

"Harold teach all people fly," Harold said happily. "Harold like teach."

"Just think. When you all know how to fly, you can all fly away from this place," Nurse Steal said.

"Harold no leave," Harold said, looking seriously at Nurse Steal. "Harold no leave Nurse Steal. Harold love Nurse Steal."

"I love you too, Harold," Nurse Steal answered, adding to herself, "far more than you will ever realize."

"You fly, we fly," Harold laughed and half raised his arms.

Bertha Shields wheeled into the dayroom with Randolph on her lap. "Come on, Harold," she called. "It's time for Sesame Street. You have to help teach Randolph how to count."

Harold followed Bertha Shields to the TV.

Nurse Steal watched Harold shuffle away. I would love to live in your simplicity if only for a few days. To live and not want has to be a great blessing she thought.

Nurse Steal was at the nurses' station as Rose Merrywood, Grace Brethren, Wilma Happy, Betty Frost and Gloria Sane made their way to their table. Down the hall she could hear George Early and Henry Right already starting to argue as they warmed up for their checker game.

The theft of her pins lay like a stone in Martha's heart, a stone that only grew heavier. She ran cold water on her hands and splashed it on her face. She dried her hands and face and rubbed a small amount of rouge on her cheeks and put on lipstick. "I must be brave," she said. "I must trust." But heading for the dayroom, she did not know if she could hold back the tears that wanted to swell up from within her.

As Martha Dearheart joined the other ladies she noticed Rose Merrywood was wearing a clean dress. She looked deep into the eyes of her friend to see if she could see any traces of guilt. She did not see any, but she supposed a jewel thief would not show guilt. She could not help but feel one of her friends had stolen her pins and decided thievery hurt both the thief and the person that had been stolen from.

"The children that were going to come and sing are not coming," Betty Frost said. "A few of them came down with mumps and they decided it would not be safe."

Grace Brethren was disappointed. "It would have been nice to see the little ones," she said.

Hazel pushed a cart into the dayroom holding colored paper, pencils, and crayons. "Would any of you ladies like to color or draw?" she asked warmly.

Only Wilma Happy asked for paper and crayons.

"I always wanted to be a painter," Wilma Happy said. "From the time I was a little girl I dreamed about being a famous painter. I wanted to travel all over the world and paint a picture of every place I had been."

"What happened?" Betty Frost asked.

"I never got around to doing it. There was always something else going on in my life."

"Do you ever regret not doing it?" Martha Dearheart asked.

"Not anymore. At times I used to, but it doesn't do one any good to think about what is past," Wilma Happy replied, taking a red crayon out of the box.

"Most of my dreams are about the past," Betty Frost said. "I find it difficult to think about the future."

"Even for the young, the future is precarious," Grace Brethren said.

Everybody around the table grew silent as if dreams of the past engulfed them.

"We need a pet dog," Betty Frost said, breaking the silence. "They are always happy and glad to see you."

"That is a wonderful idea. I will put it on the list," Martha Dearheart said.

"I read that some prisons let the inmates have pets and they have fewer problems than the prisons that don't allow pets," Wilma Happy said, taking a blue crayon out of the box.

"It makes sense," Betty Frost said.

"Sense has nothing to do with the way the modern world is heading," Martha Dearheart said.

"What are you drawing?" Rose Merrywood asked Wilma Happy.

"It's silly," Wilma Happy said. "I don't know if I want to show you, you would all laugh."

"Show us," Martha Dearheart coaxed.

"Please?" Grace Brethren said.

"In a few minutes when I am done," Wilma Happy said.

"Well then hurry," Rose Merrywood said.

"An artist cannot be rushed," Betty Frost said. "It disturbs the creative flow."

After a few minutes, Wilma Happy put all the crayons back in the box and looked at her picture. "You promise you won't laugh?" she asked.

"Promise," Grace Brethren said.

Wilma Happy held up the drawing. The picture looked like a child had drawn it. There were six older ladies, all with white hair. They were flapping their arms, and their feet were above a fluffy white cloud. Below the cloud were four multi-colored birds.

"You know it's true," Rose Merrywood gasped.

"What?" Wilma Happy asked.

"Harold can fly, you know it."

"Nobody can fly," Wilma Happy said. "I was only drawing what I hoped. I hope we can all be together forever and as free as birds."

"Can I have the picture?" Rose Merrywood asked. "I would like to put it on my wall."

"Now don't you try to jump off of the roof thinking Harold is going to teach us how to fly," Wilma Happy said with mirth in her voice.

"I won't have to," Rose Merrywood smiled back.

******

Mr. Fist was describing a lady to the men. "Just beneath her ribs her stomach flows into a graceful curve, and one can see delicate blond hairs reflecting back the light from the ocean."

"No more, no more," Robert Begone begged.

"I wonder how you get the job of taking pictures of pretty ladies," Jake Lost asked. "It really doesn't seem like it would be that hard."

"I wouldn't call that a job," Paul Mouse said. "It seems more like torture to me."

"I bet there isn't a regulation saying we can't hire a topless dancer," Robert Begone said. "I bet if we had a good attorney we could get one."

"An attorney would cost us more money than we have ever made in our lives," Mr. Fist said.

Robert Begone scratched his head and looked at his feet. "I'll be damned," he said. "I have both of my shoes on."

"Those aren't your shoes," Jake Lost said. "Those are my shoes. I wondered where my other pair of shoes went."

"Where are mine?" Robert Begone asked.

"How would I know? But I want mine back before supper."

"If I give them back I won't have any shoes," Robert Begone said.

"I will rent them to you," Jake Lost said.

"I don't have any money."

Jake Lost shook his head. "Then keep them."

Mr. Fist headed for the TV where Harold and Bertha Shields were singing along with Kermit the Frog while Bertha moved the arms of the teddy bear to the beat. Mr. Fist did not like Sesame Street so he watched George Early and Henry Right play checkers for a few minutes before heading for his room. As he passed the nurses' station he growled at Nurse Steal, "Nothing but a bunch of old people here."

Nurse Steal could not think of a reply and only nodded understandingly.

Rose Merrywood carefully placed the picture Wilma Happy had drawn on her lap and was about to push herself to her room. She wanted to hang the picture where Harold would see it. Two aides suddenly ran through the dayroom and down the west wing. Nurse Steal hurried as fast as she could behind them.

All the residents stopped doing whatever they were doing and looked in fear down the hall. Nurse Steal rushed back to the nurses' station and made a phone call. Soon the wail of an ambulance cut through the air as it sped toward Rest View. When the ambulance got to Rest View the siren was shut off. The doors at the end of the west wing, made wide enough so a stretcher could pass through without difficulty, could be heard slamming open. After a few minutes the siren came back on and slowly faded away in the distance.

Everyone knew one of the bedridden patients had died and silence settled into the corners of the dayroom.

Harold peeked tentatively into each room in the west wing before he came to the room of one of the bed ridden residents. The sheets for the bed were tossed on the floor. "Mrs. Bean gone, Mrs. Bean fly away," he said sadly with tears running down his face.

Bertha Shields stopped by the nurses' station where Nurse Steal was filling out a report that had to be submitted every time a resident died or was sent to the hospital. It was very important there were no mistakes - mistakes could incriminate the rest home for being negligent and lead to an expensive lawsuit. "Do you think Randolph will die before I do?" Bertha asked.

"Now Bertha, nobody knows when they are going to die."

"If Randolph died before me I would be all alone," Bertha Shields said.

"In all probability he won't," Nurse Steal said.

"I hope not," Bertha Shields said. "But if I die first will you promise me you will adopt Randolph?"

"I promise," Nurse Steal said. "I will love him as much as you do."

"Thank you," Bertha Shields said with relief.

An aide pushed Bertha Shields to her room.

Harold came out of the west wing. He felt troubled and wanted to ask Nurse Steal a question, but seeing she was busy he ambled listlessly around the empty dayroom. He went from window to window and then stared at the magazine rack but did not pick up a magazine. He turned off the TV and once again went from window to window.

Nurse Steal finished the report and Harold came over. "Mrs. Bean fly away. Mrs. Bean never come back, she gone," Harold said.

"Mrs. Bean has gone to heaven," Nurse Steal said.

"People in heaven fly?" he asked.

"Angels can fly," Nurse Steal said.

"Then Harold angel, Harold fly to heaven," he said and flapped toward his room.

Nurse Steal felt weary. Nurse Sly would relieve her soon but Nurse Steal knew that even at home she would feel weary.

Martha Dearheart was in her nightgown and carefully writing out the resident's recommendations. She tried to put all her thoughts into her words, but it was difficult, as she could not drive the loss of her pins out of her mind. She felt not only hurt but also outrage. So outraged she wanted to go from room to room and search everywhere. But she could not, now was not the time.

Rose Merrywood, in bed, gazed fondly at the drawing of the ladies flying. "They will believe," she said to the picture, but she wondered if it was only her deep longing that made her believe Harold could fly.

Mr. Fist took off his clothes and got into bed. "I am too tired tonight to even try and break out of this dump," he said.

Bertha Shields tucked Randolph underneath the covers. She put her ear next to his chest. "I love you," she said. "I love you," she heard Randolph answer.

Robert Begone put Jake Lost's shoes at the end of his bed. "I bet he has been the one who has been stealing my shoes and when he came to steal them again he forgot and left his own." Robert Begone laughed out loud. "That will teach him."

The room lights went out. Only the hall lights remained on and the light at the nurses' station where Nurse Sly was going over nutrition charts.

Martha Dearheart, eyes open and peering into the semi-darkness could not understand why someone she knew would steal her pins.

An old and withered hand held the two pins tightly underneath the covers, and although the person's eyes were closed, there was no sleep or peace.

After Harold felt everybody was sleeping, he slipped quietly out of bed. Tip-toeing to the window he peered into the darkness. Cocking his ear to the side he did not hear the night bird. Listening for several minutes, but still no bird, he went back to bed.

"Harold," Rose Merrywood called gently.

Harold got back out of bed, peaked around the corner of his door to make sure Nurse Sly was not looking and hurried to Rose Merrywood's room. "Why aren't you flying tonight?" Rose Merrywood asked.

"Mrs. Bean fly. Mrs. Bean angel," Harold said.

"Oh, I am glad to hear that," Rose Merrywood said.

She pointed at the picture of the flying ladies. Harold stepped back. "Beautiful, beautiful," he said in admiration

"Yes it is," Rose Merrywood said.

Harold went back to his room and got back in bed. "Fa, La, La," he heard.

"Fa, La, La," Harold sang back, but he did not get out of bed.

"Fa, La, La," the bird sang again before flying off.

Outside, by her car, Nurse Steal listened spellbound to the bird. "It is impossible," she whispered. "It has to be." But driving home there was a pleasant tingling in her stomach while the bird's song echoed in her ears.

Harold slept for several hours. Getting out of bed he opened the window. Shutting his eyes and flapping his arms he was a small brown bird with a splash of blue on its breast.

Nurse Steal was reading a romance novel. The curtains to the window were pulled back and the window was partially open. Setting the book down Nurse Steal could make out the Little Dipper. She remembered when she was a little girl and how she had loved to look at the stars, but now it seemed she never took the time to go out at night and just gaze at the night sky. When she wasn't working, she was normally perched in front of her TV or reading. She was lost in thought when she heard, "Fa, La, La."

She rushed to the window and opened it all the way. "Harold, Harold," she called, immediately feeling foolish. A small brown bird with a splash of blue on its breast landed on the window sill and sang "Fa, La, La," then flew in front of Nurse Steal's face for a few moments before disappearing into the dark. Nurse Steal stretched out her arms and began to flap them. "Fa, La, La, Fa, La, La," she sang. After a few moments she resolutely let her arms fall to her sides. She wondered where her life had gone. Where were her dreams? Now, she lived day to day putting all her wishes and hopes into her job - hiding her sadness with the sadness of the residents. "I hope I have done my best," she lamented.

Harold's feet touched the floor of his room. "Harold good boy," he said.

Across the hall Rose Merrywood held her hand over her mouth. "I knew Harold could fly, I knew," she whispered and drifted contentedly off to sleep.

Chapter Six

Martha Dearheart examined her reflection in the mirror. She was wearing a dark, navy blue dress, and black shoes, wanting to have a business look for her meeting with Mr. Dry. But the dress seemed barren without one of the pins on the collar. The empty spot where a pin should have been glared out at her with all the insecurity she now felt. "How can I succeed when somebody has stolen my heart?" she asked her reflection. But there was no answer.

Looking once more at the blaringly empty spot on her dress, she sighed deeply and picked up the recommendations.

All the residents were in the dayroom. No one was speaking as if they were all in a trance. When Martha entered the dayroom all the people looked at her in both anticipation and wariness.

Nurse Steal smiled reassuringly at Martha Dearheart. "It will be ok," she said. "There is never any harm in trying."

Martha Dearheart smiled thinly. Mr. Fist yelled, "Give him hell!"

Mr. Fist's outburst broke the trance of the residents.

"Hell!" Harold hollered.

"Booze and women!" Jake Lost called.

"Go with the armies of God!" Grace Brethren shouted, surprising Martha Dearheart. Henry Right started to chant. "We want change, we want change."

All the others joined in. "We want change. We want change."

All the apprehension was swept out of Martha Dearheart. She stood straighter, pulled her shoulders back, lifted her chin, and marched deliberately toward Mr. Dry's office.

After Martha Dearheart went into Mr. Dry's office, the residents in the dayroom were once again silent.

Mr. Dry smiled thinly at Martha Dearheart and motioned for her to sit. Mr. Dry, from behind his desk, raised his eyebrows slightly, and said simply, "yes."

Martha Dearheart rustled the papers resting on her lap, looked pleasantly at Mr. Dry and asked, "Do you like peas?"

"Let's just begin," Mr. Dry said with no humor in his voice.

"I have here a list of changes we the residents of Rest View feel should be enacted. They are not demands, they are recommendations. There is nothing out of line. I have written them out in a neat and orderly manner, mindful, I have also made a copy," Martha Dearheart said and placed the papers purposefully on Mr. Dry's desk.

Mr. Dry for a moment did nothing, as though the papers were a snake, and if he moved, the snake would strike. He then picked up the papers and quickly read over the list - his face showing no emotion either pro or con. Finished, he said to Martha Dearheart. "I will go over these in more detail tonight, and within a few days I will inform you as to the boards' decision."

"I am sure you will do what is proper," Martha Dearheart said, adding, "If you dressed more casually, the residents would like you more and not feel so intimidated by your presence. This is not a bank. You do not need a tie. This is an old folks' home. We need friends, not bosses."

After Martha Dearheart left Mr. Dry touched his tie. It seemed oppressive and truth be known he did not like wearing one.

As Martha Dearheart entered the dayroom Henry Right cheered, "Victory, victory."

"Speech, speech," George Early demanded.

"Speech, speech," Harold echoed, flapping his arms up and down.

"Mr. Dry said he would get back with me within a few days," Martha Dearheart announced.

"Strike," Jake Lost yelled. "We want action."

"A few days are not unreasonable," Martha Dearheart replied.

"What will we do if he does nothing?" Gloria Sane asked.

"We will cross that bridge when we come to it," Martha Dearheart said.

"What about our flying lessons?" Rose Merrywood asked with a worried tone in her voice.

Harold stretched out his arms and began flapping around the room.

"Fly, Harold," Jake Lost urged.

"Fa, La, La," Nurse Steal hummed to herself.

Martha Dearheart suddenly felt tired. She started for her room. "You are our champion," Henry Right called to her.

Martha Dearheart closed the door to her room even if it was against the rules. She hung her dress in the closet and sitting in her chair in her slip she began to cry. "My lovely pins, where are you?"

Harold was still flapping around the dayroom, but everybody except Rose Merrywood was ignoring him. George Early and Henry Right were playing checkers. Bertha Shields was listening to Randolph's heart, which for the last few days had seemed to her to be beating irregularly. Mr. Fist, Jake Lost, Robert Begone and Paul Mouse were engrossed in a western starring John Wayne.

The ladies were at their table. "I hope I live long enough to see the flowers bloom," Wilma Happy said, gazing at the flowerbed.

"We might not live long enough to eat lunch," Betty Frost said.

"No one dies until his or her task in life has been completed," Grace Brethren replied.

Gloria Sane scoffed, "It must be my purpose in life to live long enough to have arthritis, bursitis, diverticulitis, hardening of the arteries, heart disease, and be unable to walk."

"God's purpose for us is not always visible," Grace Brethren said.

Harold ran to the table flapping his arms. "Soon all fly," he beamed.

"It will be so wonderful," Rose Merrywood said. "So wonderful to fly away from here, such sights we will all see, such an adventure awaits us."

"Rose, I think you are finally going over the deep end," Betty Frost said.

"No. After all these years I think I finally believe in miracles," Rose Merrywood replied.

"Praise the Lord," Grace Brethren said.

"Praise the Lord," Harold said and flapped over to Mr. Fist and the other men.

Betty Shields wheeled over to the ladies. "I think Randolph is having a heart attack," she said.

Betty Frost took Randolph and proceeded to examine him. She held his left arm and counted. After a few moments she handed the teddy bear back to Bertha Shields. "He is fine," she stated confidently.

Bertha Shields sighed in relief.

"He will outlive all of us," Grace Brethren said.

Bertha Shields wheeled happily away.

Grace Brethren bowed her head and prayed silently.

Mr. Fist turned the TV off. "How come the good guy always wins?" he stormed and started to shuffle as fast as he could toward the front door. "Dive, dive," Henry Right called as the alarm went off.

Mr. Fist raced toward the parking lot. He had gone no more than twenty yards when two aides caught him by each arm. "Let me go, you communists," Mr. Fist squirmed and protested.

The two aides led Mr. Fist back to the dayroom. "It's a

record," he announced to his friends. "Almost twenty yards before I got caught."

"Did you bring back a *Playboy*?" Robert Begone asked.

"I keep telling him we need a tunnel," Paul Mouse said. "The direct approach will never work."

Harold started flapping his arms. "I know, it's our only hope," Mr. Fist said.

"Fly, fly," Harold said.

"How can anyone believe in hope?" Robert Begone asked.

"You have to hope," Jake Lost said.

"Please hope," Harold almost whimpered.

Robert Begone looked at his shoeless feet. "I hope somebody brings my shoes back," he said.

"When we all learn how to fly, you won't need those damn shoes," Jake Lost said, taking his hearing aid out of his ear.

"And you won't need that hearing aid," Paul Mouse said.

"What?" Jake Lost bellowed.

"Fly, fly, fly," Harold said and started flapping in circles around the men.

"I bet I can make it twenty-five yards next time," Mr. Fist said.

Rose Merrywood watched Harold and touched her withered legs. Oh Harold, she thought. I do hope you teach us how to fly soon. I have so little time.

Henry Right scattered his checkers onto the floor. "You cheating bastard," he shouted at George Early.

"Maybe someday you will learn how to play checkers," George Early laughed.

"I'll play you after lunch for tonight's dessert," Henry Right challenged.

"What if I don't like what is for dessert?" George Early asked.

"It's the winning that counts," Henry Right said.

"Even if I don't like it, if I win it from you it will be delicious," George Early said.

The residents slowly emptied the dayroom. When everyone was gone Harold, flapping his arms, approached Nurse Steal.

"Fa, La, La," Nurse Steal sang to him.

Harold stopped flapping his arms. He tilted his head to one side and a large grin erupted on his face. "Nurse Steal fly?" he asked seriously.

Nurse Steal spread out her arms and flapped them several times. "Nurse Steal needs lessons," Harold said.

"I will come," Nurse Steal said.

"Fa, La, La," Harold sang and hugged Nurse Steal. "Harold love Nurse Steal, Harold good boy."

Martha Dearheart put on a bright red dress for supper. "They must never see me cry. I am needed," she said.

A person held the two pins up to the sunlight, both admiring them and feeling sad, before placing the pins gently underneath the mattress.

Paul Mouse pushed his mashed potatoes around on the plate, but could not make himself take a bite. The carrots, he had slowly shoved on the floor, and the piece of ham, now cold, looked like it was halfway to becoming jerky. Mr. Fist and the others had devoured their lunch as though they had not eaten in a month. They were looking stuffed and content. Paul Mouse headed toward his room without talking to anybody. "You should eat," Robert Begone called after him. "Strange things happen to people when they don't eat."

Paul Mouse sat in his chair. It was quiet with everybody in the dining room - a quiet that he liked. At night there were sighs and moans that echoed down the hall. Paul Mouse remembered how he used to enjoy the quiet evenings when he and his wife would take walks. Thinking about his wife, he felt deeply saddened for a moment. He had never wanted her to die first. He had always wanted to die first. She had been such a caring and gentle lady. But it seemed to Paul Mouse it was always the kind and gentle who died first. Maybe God wanted to bring them to his side and ask them how they could be so caring when the world he had created for them was nothing but futility. "It is not a blessing to get old," Paul Mouse said.

Paul Mouse scratched his head and then his leg. It was a beautiful day outside. He went over to the window and opened it as far as he could then bent his head down to feel the slight breeze that drifted into the room. Paul breathed deeply the fresh air and lay on his bed. Putting his head wearily on the pillow there was a crinkling sound from underneath the pillow. Sticking his hand tentatively under the pillow he felt a magazine. Paul Mouse got out of bed, picked up the pillow, and almost yelled looking at the scantily dressed blond on the cover licking an ice cube that was shaped like a rabbit. He started pacing anxiously back and forth across the room. "Who could have done this?" he questioned. He put the magazine back under his pillow and ran as fast as he could out of the room. Halfway down the hall he met Mr. Fist and Jake Lost. "You look like you have seen a ghost," Mr. Fist said.

Paul Mouse was so excited that when he tried to speak all that came out were croaking sounds.

Robert Begone caught up with the men. "You look weird and sound weirder," he said to Paul Mouse who was scratching himself madly still unable to speak.

The three men started to walk away when Paul Mouse blurted, "I've, I've, I've seen a naked woman."

Robert Begone scowled. "I told you, you should eat, people hallucinate when they don't eat."

The three men left Paul Mouse standing in the hall.

Back in his room, Paul peeked under his pillow and the *Playboy* was still there.

Nurse Steal was going over her paperwork when Mr. Dry came by carrying Martha Dearheart's recommendations. "I'm going home early," he told her.

Nurse Steal was worried Mr. Dry would do nothing with the recommendations except send them off to his superiors, who really had no idea as to what really went on at Rest View, they were only concerned with the bottom line, not the lives of the people they controlled.

Nurse Steal made her rounds. To her surprise Harold was even sleeping. The only person who was not sleeping was Paul Mouse. "Are you feeling ok?" Nurse Steal asked.

"I haven't felt this good in years," Paul Mouse replied with a mischievous grin.

After her rounds Nurse Steal stood by the large window the ladies always sat by. The freshly planted marigolds were almost ready to open. She could hear the songs of birds enjoying the nice day. "Fa, La, La," she hummed.

About to turn, she heard, "Fa, La, La," and saw a small drab brown bird with mystical red eyes in the flowerbed. For some reason the bird seemed to radiate age and wisdom. "Fa, La, La," the bird sang before flying away.

Going back to the nurses' station Nurse Steal felt light on her feet.

The red eyed bird darted around the rest home and landed in the redbud tree outside of Harold's window. "Fa, La, La," the bird sang.

Waking immediately Harold hurried over to the window.

"Fa, La, La," the bird sang again.

"No fly now," Harold said. "Harold rest. Harold give flying lessons."

"Fa, La, La," the bird beckoned.

"No, Harold rest. Harold must teach hope."

The bird seemed to smile at Harold before flying off.

"Hope, hope," Harold said. "Must teach hope."

******

Mr. Fist, Jake Lost, and Robert Begone were sitting by the magazine rack waiting for Paul Mouse. "Where is he?" Robert Begone asked, trying not to show he was worried.

"He is never this late," Jake Lost said, also worried.

"He has never hallucinated naked women before, either," Mr. Fist said, also worried.

"He might be stealing my shoes," Robert Begone said.

"I am going to get some glue and glue your shoes on your feet," Jake Lost told Robert Begone.

Paul Mouse shuffled up to the men looking at them like he was the only kid on the block who had a football.

All the men did not show how glad they were to see him and that they had been worried.

"Are there any new magazines?" Paul Mouse asked.

"No," Mr. Fist answered. "It will have to be a rerun day."

Paul Mouse reached into his shirt pocket and handed a folded up page from a magazine to Mr. Fist.

Mr. Fist unfolded the page slowly and hollered, "Jackpot! Jackpot!"

Jake Lost leaned over and even with his bad eyes said in wonderment, "It really is a naked woman."

Robert Begone grabbed the page and looking toward the heavens said, "Blessed be those who wait."

The four men started to laugh like four drunks who knew they would get in trouble with their wives but really didn't care. Harold, on his way to watch Sesame Street, hearing the laughter, flapped over to the men.

Harold looked at the picture and sang, "Hope, hope, hope."

"Describe her in detail," Robert Begone begged.

Harold, seeing Bertha Shields and Randolph, flapped his way toward the TV.

Rose Merrywood, Grace Brethren, Martha Dearheart, Betty Frost, and Wilma Happy were intently watching the four men. "I wonder what evil thing they are all excited about?" Grace Brethren asked.

"Whatever it is, they all have seemed to get a lot of vigor in the last few minutes," Rose Merrywood said.

"Probably some stupid football or baseball magazine," Betty Frost said.

"The only reason they would ever watch sports would be to see the ladies on the sidelines making spectacles of themselves," Grace Brethren said.

"I wish they had men who stood on the sidelines dressed in tiny briefs," Rose Merrywood said.

"Me too," Wilma Happy said.

Grace Brethren changed the subject. "Do you think Mr. Dry will grant us any of our requests?" she asked Martha Dearheart, who seemed to look tired and distant. "Are you feeling well?" Grace Brethren added.

"I'm ok," Martha Dearheart said. "As to your question, I

don't see any reason he could turn down any of our requests, but I really don't know the laws or insurance regulations they have to follow. Maybe this is one time we are all going to have to depend on God."

For some reason Grace Brethren did not comment.

******

Mr. Dry was glad to be home before his wife and children. He went directly to his den, sat at his desk, and lay Martha Dearheart's papers in front of him. He said to the papers, "You people don't understand. It is not me who has robbed you of your dignity. But, maybe I have helped by becoming complacent. We have all become slaves to our own needs. I think I have ignored you as people and only thought of my family's security."

Mr. Dry read the recommendations again.

Dear Mr. Dry:

As I have put myself in the position of spokeswoman for the residents of Rest View, I truly want you to understand that in no way am I admonishing you or your staff for our conditions. Life has taught me much about understanding. We are not cold of heart, age has not made us cynical or bitter - at least not to the point we are not caring and considerate human beings. Please know I am not your enemy, merely an opponent. With this aside, these are our recommendations, but there could be more.

Number 1. We are members of the human race. We are not animals that have reached the end of our usefulness and have been left to die in some barren pasture on the edge of a farm. Although we are wards, it is not necessary for our keepers to wear uniforms like jailers. So, please, let the nurses and aides wear clothes that do not make us feel like we are in an institution.

Number 2. Being that it is the innate function of all human beings to produce and be around living things, I recommend the residents of Rest View be able to have plants in their rooms under our care and a small plot outside where we could plant flowers and vegetables. Life is watching life. Also, please get rid of the fake plants in the dayroom and replace them with real ones.

Number 3. We would like a birdbath to be placed outside at the end of the east wing, along with chairs so we can sit and watch the birds. For some reason, bird mania has been sweeping through Rest View and heaven knows it would be better than TV.

Number 4. I can see no reason why there could not be a dog or cat that could roam Rest View. The source of solace and pleasure that pets produce is beyond words.

Number 5. There are many old men in our home. For good or bad, these men want a subscription to *Playboy*. They would not be allowed to bring the magazine to the dayroom.

But, who cares if they look.

Number 6. Some people would like a drink of alcohol every so often. The staff could dole it out. Besides, at our age a little booze never hurt anybody.

Number 7. Harold, bless his soul, thinks he can fly and wants to teach all the residents to fly. The residents want an organized class taught by Harold on How to Fly. If nothing else, it gives them exercise and a fantasy to believe in.

Number 8. I feel we should be able to close our doors all the way.

Number 9. There is no need for a buzzer on the front door. Rest View is not a prison nor do we live in a submarine.

Number 10. Mr. Fist would like to go fishing.

Number 11. I feel people should be able to go outside without being escorted by a nurse or an aide.

In closing, I want you to remember, Mr. Dry, you too will grow old. If it is a blessing, I do not know. If you are a lucky person you will not die in a rest home feeling alone and abandoned.

Respectfully,
Martha Dearheart.

Mr. Dry went to the backyard. In the corner, by a wooden fence, was a bed of blue irises. A stone walk led to a barbeque pit. "I have always thought about growing old," Mr. Dry said out loud. "I have dreamed of sitting on my porch, old and tired, contemplating my life and hoping in all things possible that I have done the right thing for people and my family, but knowing that most of my decisions have been wrong and motivated by job and security. I don't know if I can give you dignity. I might have forgotten what it is.

Chapter Seven

All the residents were in their rooms for the night. Nurse Steal did not feel like going home and she and Nurse Sly were in the kitchen making coffee.

"I ran into an old friend of mine who graduated from nursing school the same time I did," Nurse Sly said. "She is working at a hospital and getting twice the money we are. I am thinking about applying for a job. Besides needing the money I don't know if my heart can take it anymore working here."

"It's hard for rest homes to hire enough people to give people proper care," Nurse Steal said, understanding now that even if she did not like Nurse Sly, Nurse Sly had a caring heart, which made Nurse Steal feel guilty.

"It's appalling," Nurse Sly said.

"It's a disgrace," Nurse Steal said. "I think this country is going to have to nationalize our health and elderly care. There is no way many people can afford to grow old."

"Leave it to America to teach the world everything has to have a price," Nurse Sly said.

"I gave up on ever trying getting ahead," Nurse Steal said, forcing a wry grin.

"If Harold weren't here you would leave," Nurse Sly said.

Nurse Steal did not respond to the question, but asked, "If

you leave for a better paying job, could you forget these people?"

"No, I doubt it. Everyday when I see them I see myself when I am old."

"Me either. I guess that is why I stay. I keep telling myself it will all get better, but it just rolls on the same old way, understaffed, underpaid, and here I am, moving through my days trying to make people feel better when I can't even make myself feel better."

The front door buzzer blared, within thirty seconds an aide ran out the front door. "Mr. Fist," Nurse Steal called as she headed for the dayroom

But it was not Mr. Fist. Mr. Fist was looking at the picture of a lady Paul Mouse had given him.

Robert Begone was not hard to catch, nor was he hard to turn around and direct back toward the front door. When the aide had Robert Begone back inside, Nurse Steal escorted him back to his room. "I made it to the parking lot," he said proudly. "I beat Mr. Fist's record."

"Yes you did," Nurse Steal replied with a smile.

Feeling lonely Nurse Steal decided to check on a few of the residents. Bertha Shields was asleep and Randolph was propped up in a chair with an open book in his lap. Grace Brethren was reading her Bible so Nurse Steal did not disturb her. Paul Mouse was sleeping sounder than she ever remembered and she smiled at his small scrawny face wrinkled into a satisfied smile. Rose Merrywood was in bed with her reading light on but was not reading. "Hello," Rose Merrywood said pleasantly.

Nurse Steal pulled the covers up around Rose's neck. "You know Harold flies, don't you?" Rose Merrywood said.

"It would be very hard to believe, Rose," Nurse Steal said, but still confused by Harold's singing the same exact song the bird with a splash of blue on his breast sang.

"He flaps his arms and he flies away," Rose Merrywood said.

"Why does he come back?" Nurse Steal asked.

"This is his home. He has nowhere else to go."

"We all need a home," Nurse Steal said trying to sound

upbeat.

"This is not my home. When I learn to fly I will never come back. Never," Rose Merrywood said emphatically.

"I wouldn't either," Nurse Steal said.

Nurse Steal looked into Harold's room. Harold was sleeping. His tennis shoes were under his bed and his bib overalls were folded neatly over his chair. "Oh, Harold," she half prayed. "If you can fly, fly away, fly far away before this place takes everything from you."

Nurse Steal went into Jake Lost's room and turned off his hearing aid.

Passing Wilma Happy's room, she heard faint sobs. Wilma Happy had her pillow over her face trying to quiet her sobs. "Why are you crying?" Nurse Steal asked gently picking up the pillow.

"I am lonely," Wilma Happy cried.

Nurse Steal stroked Wilma Happy's cheek, but could not think of anything to say. She held her hand until Wilma drifted off to sleep. She then said with a heavy heart, "We are all lonely."

Nurse Steal went to the rooms of all of the bedridden patients - all the people past loneliness, or caring, or knowing, or loving. She did not feel the empathy she felt for the people who could still think and feel. These people were already with God. Nurse Steal did not believe in hell, life was hell - all people who tried to be good in this life went to heaven. Those who had made a mockery of being alive went to oblivion. A good and caring God would not curse anybody to time eternal in hell.

Nurse Steal got her handbag from the nurses' station. Nurse Sly, reading a medical journal, looked up and with a distant smile said, "See you in the morning."

"If I don't fly away," Nurse Steal replied.

Nurse Steal put her handbag in the car. She then snuck around Rest View and hid behind a tree where she could see Harold's window. "Fly Harold, let me see you fly," she said hopefully.

She waited for over an hour, but nothing happened, and she disappointedly went back to her car. Starting the engine, she did not hear the little bird perched in the redbud tree outside Harold's window singing softly, "Fa, La, La."

Nor did she see Harold get out of bed and sing, "Fa, La, La," as he started to flap his arms.

But Rose Merrywood heard the song and smiled. "Fly for all of us. Fly and bring back dreams from the stars."

Harold stopped flapping his arms and peered out the window. He saw the shadowed bird. "Harold no fly until teach," he whispered and went back to bed.

******

Martha Dearheart woke up with a start. It had been a terrible dream. A skeletal hand with her pearl pin in his palm had appeared in her dream, but as Martha reached for the pin the hand moved barely out of her reach - try as she may Martha could not grab the pin. Martha Dearheart turned on her reading light. "I know we are not supposed to be chained to our possessions," she begged. "I know if I was true of heart and spirit the theft of what I love would not bother me. Others have lost more than I have. Why cannot I forgive and forget?"

Turning the light off Martha Dearheart closed her eyes, but the garnet and pearl pins floated in her mind's eye. "Dear Lord, I hope the person who stole them need them more than I do," she prayed.

In another room a person clutched the two pins tightly in their hand. "Forgive me," the person lamented. "Please forgive me?"

******

Martha Dearheart, although looking calm, felt nervous. Mr. Dry had informed Nurse Steal he wanted to see Martha Dearheart right after lunch. "It's D-Day," Martha Dearheart replied to Nurse Steal after being told the news. She did not want the other residents to know, but it did not work - all the residents were waiting in the dayroom and gave Martha Dearheart imploring looks as she entered Mr. Dry's office.

Smiling warmly at Martha Dearheart Mr. Dry shut the door

and sat at his desk. Martha Dearheart remained standing. "I have looked over your recommendations carefully. I trust you know this," Mr. Dry said, not telling Martha he had not consulted the owners of Rest View and, in fact, he was going out on a limb by making the decisions by himself.

"I think you are an honorable man," Martha Dearheart said, adding, with a sly grin, "You look much more comfortable without a tie on."

"I also want you to know I do not like peas," Mr. Dry said.

"They are disgusting," Martha said.

"Now, to your recommendations, first off, the staff will still wear their uniforms," Mr. Dry began in a professional tone. "As to real plants, you can have plants in your rooms and we will replace the artificial plants in the dayroom with real ones. I also see no reason why those of you who are able should not be allowed to have a small flower and vegetable garden. I have ordered a birdbath, and extra chairs will be put by the east window. There can be no pets and no men's magazines and no fishing. We also cannot remove the buzzer from the door and residents cannot go outside without being accompanied by an aide or a nurse. Now, as to flying lessons, Harold can hold a class once a day for no longer than thirty minutes. We do not want the residents to be overtaxed."

"Did you ever dream about flying?" Martha Dearheart asked.

"Only when I was a child," Mr. Dry answered.

"Maybe that is our main problem. We no longer think like children," Martha Dearheart said.

"Also, you can shut your doors but not lock them, "Mr. Dry said, wishing there was a small portion of a child remaining in him. "I suppose a few seconds longer for a nurse to get into a room if there is an emergency does not make a huge difference."

Martha Dearheart smiled.

Mr. Dry opened the door for Martha Dearheart. "You are a good man," Martha Dearheart said. "Thank you."

She had not gone more than a few feet when she remembered asking for whiskey, and she turned.

"No booze," Mr. Dry said shaking his head, "unless it is brought by a relative and consumed while they are visiting."

During Martha Dearheart's time in the office the residents were as quiet as people at a political convention who knew their candidate did not have a chance of winning. When Martha Dearheart entered the dayroom there was no cheering, only looks of apprehension.

Martha Dearheart felt a pang of remorse shoot through her knowing one of the residents had her pins, and for a moment she felt bitter and alienated, but she forced the feelings from her. "Good news or bad news first?" Martha Dearheart asked.

"Bad news," everyone answered.

"First, for Mr. Fist and his band of merry men there will be no *Playboy* or fishing and you still must ask permission to go outdoors."

To her surprise Mr. Fist and his crew only smiled at her.

"For Henry Right and George Early. Forget the booze unless a relative brings it to you and you drink it with them."

Once again there was no protest.

"There will be no pets."

The ladies murmured sadly to themselves, but the men did not seem to care one way or the other.

"The nurses and aides will still wear their uniforms."

"At least we know who the enemy is," Jake Lost said.

"Nurse Steal no enemy," Harold said.

"No, we all love Nurse Steal," Jake Lost apologized.

Nurse Steal smiled.

"How about dancing girls?' Henry Right asked.

"I forgot to ask," Martha Dearheart confessed.

"That's ok, one day Grace Brethren will dance for us," Mr. Fist said, grinning.

Grace Brethren ignored the remark.

"Now for the good news," Martha Dearheart said. "We will be able to have plants in our rooms and a small vegetable and flower garden, and the fake plants in the dayroom will be replaced with real plants."

"Thank you, God," Grace Brethren sighed.

Betty Frost smiled. She pictured in her mind a row of yellow snapdragons and a cluster of pumpkin orange poppies.

"We will also have a birdbath by the window."

"Bird, bird," Harold shouted happily.

We can close our doors but not lock them."

A sigh went through the dayroom.

"And last but not least, Harold will be able to give us flying lessons every day for thirty minutes."

A roar erupted from the residents, all except Grace Brethren, who muttered, "As I stated before, I will take no part in such foolishness."

Harold started skipping around the dayroom flapping his arms and shouting, "Fly, fly, fly. We all fly."

"Fa, La, La," Rose Merrywood sang, holding back tears.

"We'll break out of this joint now," Mr. Fist hollered.

Harold completed another circle around the room and then flapped to his room where he looked anxiously at the redbud tree.

"There is nothing else," Martha Dearheart said.

The residents applauded.

George Early poked Henry Right in the arm. "How long before the brew is ready?" he asked.

"Soon," Henry Right whispered back.

"You did very well," Nurse Steal said to Martha Dearheart.

"Better than I expected," Martha Dearheart replied and headed for her room.

George Early and Henry Right started playing checkers. Mr. Fist and his crew were in the corner looking like they were scheming over something. Rose Merrywood, Grace Brethren, Betty Frost, Wilma Happy, and Gloria Sane were at their table. Nurse Steal was happy for the residents but wished she could do away with her uniform and wear something that had a little color to it.

Rose Merrywood was more excited than she had been in years thinking about flying.

"I think we should have Nurse Steal bring us a seed catalog," Grace Brethren said.

"Oh, pooh on the flowers," Rose Merrywood said. "By the time they start to come up we will all be able to fly out of here anyway."

"You keep thinking like that and they will take you to the funny farm," Grace Brethren said.

"This is the funny farm," Rose Merrywood retorted. "And I know Harold can fly," she added and spun her chair around and wheeled toward her room as fast as she could.

As Rose Merrywood passed Harold's door, she stopped. Harold was standing by the window and she could see a small brown bird with vivid red eyes in the redbud tree. She could not make out what Harold was saying, but she could hear his voice. It looked as though the bird was listening intently to his every word. Harold turned and flapped his arms several times. "Bird happy, bird say ok teach all friends fly. Bird say better to be free," Harold smiled. "But bird say people must hope or no fly."

"Oh, Harold. I don't know if anyone will believe us," Rose Merrywood said.

"Rose believe," Harold said.

"I do so believe. I just don't know if I have the strength to fly."

"Old birds fly too," Harold said matter of factly.

"I never thought of that," Rose Merrywood said happily.

Both Harold and Rose Merrywood held out their arms and flapped them a few times. "Fa, La, La," Harold sang as Rose Merrywood went to her room and Harold headed back to the dayroom.

Rose Merrywood tried to decide what type of bird she would be when she learned how to fly. She could not decide between a robin, a wren, or a meadowlark.

Paul Mouse handed Mr. Fist another folded up page out of his *Playboy*. Mr. Fist tried to calm his hands as he unfolded the paper. It took all of Mr. Fist's descriptive powers to describe the beautiful girl. When he was done, he handed the page back to Paul Mouse. The four men were dumbfounded. "I don't know if I can take this much excitement in one day," Jake Lost said.

"The old biblical kings had six or seven women that slept

with them to keep them warm," Robert Begone said.

"We should have made that one of our demands," Paul Mouse said.

"Seems only right," Mr. Fist agreed.

A van pulled into the parking lot. In the front seat was a man who was obviously bothered. In the back, a lady, with tears in her eyes, held the hand of a wheelchair bound old woman. The old woman seemed to have no life left in her. Her eyes were dull and she slumped in the wheel chair like she was no more than a lump of clay. "Oh mommy," the lady cried. "I am so sorry, but we cannot care for you anymore."

Two aides lifted the old woman out of the van and pushed her into Rest View, followed by the lady. The man did not get out of the van. The old woman was left by the nurses' station and the lady was escorted to Mr. Dry's office. Bertha Shields and Randolph were in the dayroom, and seeing the woman, Bertha Shields wheeled over. Harold joined them. The woman looked vacantly at Bertha Shields. "This is Randolph," Bertha Shields said, holding up the teddy bear.

"Carrie! Carrie! Carrie!" the woman screamed in a voice that was so shrill Bertha Shields and Harold covered their ears. Her daughter, hearing the screams, ran from Mr. Dry's office and out to the van and back. "Here she is," the daughter said, handing the woman a Raggedy Ann doll with curly orange hair and a blue print dress. The woman stopped screaming and stroked the cheeks of the doll as if she was wiping away tears. Bertha Shields held up Randolph once again. "Look, you have somebody to play with now," she said.

The woman held up the doll for Bertha Shields and Randolph to see. "She is a fine and healthy baby," the woman said with little emotion. "Her name is Carrie."

"And who are you?" Bertha Shields asked.

"It no longer matters," the woman answered with a hopeless look in her eyes.

"Randolph is sick a lot," Bertha Shields said.

The woman did not reply.

A few minutes later an aide pushed the woman to her room,

followed by Mr. Dry and the daughter. When the daughter came back through the dayroom she was crying.

Harold went to the new lady's room. The lady was holding her doll and staring blankly at the wall. "Harold teach Carrie fly," Harold said. "Carrie make good bird."

The lady did not look at Harold.

"Must hope, only hope left," he said softly.

The woman gave Harold an empty look and did not reply.

******

Martha Dearheart felt amazingly good about the small accomplishments she had an instrumental role in arranging. If there was nothing earth shattering about what had transpired, at least there had been some headway. She knew she could not stop the rest home problem altogether, no more than she could stop people from getting sick. But, at least, for the moment, it took some of the pain away over her stolen pins.

Martha Dearheart was surprised when a pick up truck drove by her window with a young man in the back steadying a large concrete birdbath. She went out into the hall and toward the east window where all the residents had already gathered. Two men unloaded the birdbath and one went and got a bucket of water and filled it. As he did the residents applauded and he smiled and waved. "There's a treat for your birds," Mr. Fist told Harold. Harold was so overjoyed all he could do was giggle.

Seeing Harold's simple joy, Martha Dearheart did her best not to cry, but still her eyes grew damp. Nurse Steal and Hazel were behind the group of people. No sooner had the truck left than several birds flew to the bath. The birds put on a great show of jumping in and out of the water.

Flapping his arms, Harold skipped up the hall as fast as he could. "Don't let him get so tired he can't teach us how to fly," Mr. Fist told Nurse Steal.

The residents drifted back to their rooms for their afternoon nap. "If Hazel is here we probably have to play bingo tonight," George Early said to Henry Right. "I don't think we have a chance as long as Randolph can play."

"Maybe fortified we do," Henry Right winked.

"Is it ready?" George Early asked excitedly.

"When everybody is in their room, come by."

George Early went to his room and waited anxiously for close to twenty minutes. Looking down the hall cautiously and seeing nobody, he raced his wheelchair to Henry Right's room.

A few minutes later Mr. Fist also peered out of his door. Instead of waiting for dark, he was going to make a daring daylight attempt at escape. He dashed for the dayroom. As he neared the door he was already growing tired, and it took all of his strength to push the door open. The buzzer sounded. Robert Begone, down for his nap, smiled. "You will not beat my record, Mr. Fist," he said confidently.

Mr. Fist was four paces from the parking lot when the aides caught up with him. "Ten bucks for five more yards," Mr. Fist pleaded.

When they got back to the dayroom, Robert Begone was by the nurses' station. "Good try," he said to Mr. Fist.

Mr. Fist stuck his tongue out at him.

"Still the champ," Robert Begone told Nurse Steal.

The distraction was what Henry Right and George Early needed. They each had a glass filled with an amber liquid with particles of raisins and prunes floating in it. "Looks good," Henry Right said. The men clinked their glasses together and took large swallows.

"It's terrible," George Early coughed.

"Not fit for a dog," Henry Right sputtered.

But when the burning subsided they took another swallow.

Ten minutes later, and after another glass, the men were passed out. Henry's Rights head was flopped to one side and his tongue was protruding from his mouth. George Early slumped in his chair like his body was made from jello.

Fifteen minutes later, Grace Brethren, going by the room and seeing the comatose men, screamed. Nurse Steal ran to the room, saw the two glasses, and the jar of amber liquid, and knew what had happened. She smelled the liquid and made a sour face and poured the home brew down the toilet. With the help of two aides she got the men into their beds. Searching Henry Right's room she found the other jars and disposed of them.

When Henry Right woke up, it was dark. He had missed bingo. Randolph won the first and third game, but George Early, no worse for wear, won the second game. Unlike George Early, Henry Right felt like his head was a throbbing drum that would never stop pounding. He got into his wheelchair and wheeled toward the end of the hall. The light from the hall spread beyond the birdbath. He wished he was a bird and could jump into the cool water, but he couldn't and he began to cry softly. He did not really know why he cried. He did not know if it was because he was old, crippled and useless, or if it was because his life had seemed to go by so quickly, or for his dear and departed wife - whatever the reason, his tears fell in tiny unseen streams. As he cried, he saw a small brown bird with hypnotizing red eyes land on the birdbath. For some reason Henry Right stopped crying and he wheeled his chair closer to the window. The bird gazed at him. His red eyes bore into the very center of Henry Right's heart and seemed to say, "Don't cry, everything will work out."

The bird jumped into the water, splashed around, and jumped back out, making Henry Right laugh.

"Fa, La, La," the bird sang.

Henry Right stuck out his arms and started flapping them. "Fa, La, La," the bird sang.

Henry flapped his arms faster.

"Fa, La, La, Fa, La, La," the bird sang.

With the next flap, Henry Right felt his rear come out of the wheelchair at least an inch. The sensation scared him so badly he let out a bone-curdling scream.

The bird darted off.

Nurse Sly ran down the hall and met Henry Right wheeling his chair as fast as he could and yelling, "By God, we can do it! We can do it! We can do it!"

"Be calm," Nurse Sly ordered.

"We can do it! We can do it!" Henry Right hollered again.

"It will be ok," Nurse Sly soothed as she pushed him back to his room.

She helped him into bed and put a cool wash cloth on his forehead. "If I had not done it I would have never believed it," Henry Right said to Nurse Sly.

"Done what?" Nurse Sly asked.

Henry Right started to tell her, but had second thoughts. "You tell Harold I know," he said. "Tell him I know."

Harold was awake and listening to every word. When Nurse Sly left, he went over to Henry Right's room. Henry Right's eyes wide open like he had just seen the face of God and would never shut his eyes again. He grabbed Harold's arm. "I flew, Harold," he said. "But I had better not tell anyone."

"Fa, La, La," Harold sang.

"Fa, La, La," Henry Right sang.

Harold stretched out his arms and flapped them several times.

"I have to learn how to land and take off," Henry Right said. "You have to start your lessons soon."

Harold went back to his room and by the window he flapped his arms quickly. His feet came several inches off the floor and then settled back.

Nurse Sly filled out a report. I strongly recommend that Mr. Right be put under psychological examination she wrote.

Henry Right's outburst woke Martha Dearheart and she could not go back to sleep. She put on her robe and slippers and went to see Nurse Sly.

"Martha, what in the world are you doing out of bed?" Nurse Sly asked.

"I think I need a man," Martha Dearheart joked.

Nurse Sly smiled. "Would you like to drink a cup of coffee with me in the kitchen?"

"That would be nice."

*****

A person made their way slowly to Martha Dearheart's room and gently placed a garnet pin and a pearl pin on the pillow. The person looked longingly at them for a few moments and started to leave, but then stopped, and picking up the garnet pin went back to their room.

******

"You like Nurse Steal, don't you?" Nurse Sly asked Martha Dearheart as she poured the coffee.

"Nurse Steal is loved by most of us," Martha Dearheart answered.

"You all don't like me as much," Nurse Sly said sadly.

"No, but we respect you."

"It is not the same," Nurse Sly said with a slight smile.

"You have a tough job and you hide your feelings," Martha Dearheart said.

"I think I have found another job at a children's hospital," Nurse Sly said.

"That would be harder than working here. It would be harder to understand when they die," Martha Dearheart said.

"I have thought of that," Nurse Sly said sadly. "At least here we expect death."

"I have no doubt you will be good with children. I know you are very caring," Martha Dearheart said.

"I fear growing old," Nurse Sly said. "Working here I see what I will become and it scares me."

"You can't fear what you cannot avoid," Martha Dearheart said.

"I know, but it does no good," Nurse Sly said.

They talked a little while longer about nothing really important and with the coffee finished Martha Dearheart went back to her room. She immediately saw the pearl pin on her pillow. With trembling fingers she picked up the pin and held it over her heart. "Thank you, thank you, I know you need but I also need," she sighed with relief.

She fixed the pin to her nightgown and went to bed. She dreamed she was home with her son - her son who looked so proud in his Navy uniform.

In another room a hand was clenched around the garnet pin as eyes peered into the darkness. The darkness did not seem as dark or the loneliness as deep holding the jewel.

******

Waking up early Grace Brethren thought about her father who had been a preacher. A strict man so inflamed by God he had never shown his children real love. Love was reading the Bible or a whipping at the slightest infraction of a rule. She thought about her mother - a serious woman that never smiled or praised her children. Grace held no love for either her father or her mother. She forced herself to respect them, if only for the reason they had given her life. Grace remembered being a young girl and how she dreamed about living in a home with a husband that was merry and happy. She dreamed about dancing and going to parties. But it had never happened. She did not know if it was the will of her father that had finally won over her own will or the fact maybe she had given up on her own dreams. For whatever reason she had spent her life alone, never seeking love, only the words of the Bible, but the Bible had never truly given her satisfaction in life. She had taught math, English, and religion, at an all girls' school in Minnesota until she retired. After retiring she worked tirelessly for the church until her health began to fail. Now there was a void in her that prayers did not fill. An emptiness that wanted to be hugged and kissed and told she was beautiful. But she had pushed dancing and merriment from her life as if it was a sin, and now she wondered if she had been right. Was it a sin to dance? Was it a sin to love and long for the touch of another? If it was, she wished she had sinned more in her life.

Chapter Eight

Nurse Steal informed Harold he could give his first flying lesson would be right after breakfast. "Harold try hard. All must hope. Harold not want to be bad boy," Harold told Nurse Steal.

"Don't worry, no matter what, you will never be a bad boy," Nurse Steal replied.

"Nurse Steal must come," Harold implored.

"Fa, La, La," Nurse Steal sang.

Before breakfast Mr. Dry told Nurse Steal he wanted her to monitor the flying lessons. He also inquired as to the new resident. "All she does is gaze at the bare wall and hold her doll," Nurse Steal informed him. "She does not want to leave her room nor will she talk. We have been taking her meals to her. She doesn't eat everything but she does eat."

"Hopefully, in time, she will want to meet the other people," Mr. Dry replied. He also mentioned Nurse Sly's report about recommending psychological monitoring of Henry Right, but he did not think it was necessary.

Nurse Steal and a nervous Harold were standing in front of all the gathered people. All except Grace Brethren, who was sitting alone in the back of the room having informed everyone again she would not participate in such foolishness. The people in wheelchairs were in the front with their chairs far enough apart they could flap their arms, while those that could stand either by themselves or with walkers were behind and to either side.

"Ladies and gentlemen, Harold has been kind enough to volunteer his time to teach us all how to fly. I give everybody, Harold," Nurse Steal announced.

The people applauded politely and with the applause Harold was no longer nervous. He looked at Grace Brethren, "Please fly," he begged.

She shook her head.

Martha Dearheart wanted to say something to her but she did not.

"Come on, Grace," Rose Merrywood coaxed.

Grace Brethren shook her head again.

Harold shut his eyes and started to hum. A hum that was a gentle wave and at first caught the residents by surprise, but when Harold continued humming they felt the tone covering them - covering them in a soft blanket of sound that returned them to a younger time in their lives. Harold hummed and it was like he was a small child, too young yet to know how to formulate words, but the sound was filled with all of life's promise and hopes.

When Harold stopped humming, everyone felt at peace. He stretched out his arms and started flapping them slowly. "Fa, La, La," he sang.

"Fa, La, La," the residents sang back, flapping their arms.

"Please let me fly?" Rose Merrywood begged.

"I can do it. I can do it," Henry Right told himself.

"Further than the parking lot," Mr. Fist said.

"We are all a bunch of idiots," Robert Begone said but still flapped his arms.

Harold went to each resident and in a beseeching voice said, "Must hope, must hope."

Bertha Shields was holding the arms of Randolph and moving them up and down. "Randolph fly," Harold said to her.

Mr. Fist started flapping his arms so fast it looked like he was swatting at a swarm of mosquitoes. "Whoopee!" he shouted.

Nurse Steal moved her large arms up and down slowly.

Grace Brethren watched them with a disgusted look on her face. By the time Harold had circled the room twice Nurse Steal noticed some of the residents were growing tired. "Enough for today," she announced. "We can't expect to fly in one lesson."

Harold lowered his arms and everybody followed suit. "Good, soon all fly," he said.

"That was great fun," Rose Merrywood said to Martha Dearheart.

"Yes it was," Martha Dearheart agreed, touching her pearl pin.

"I tell you, I thought for a moment my feet came off the ground," Mr. Fist told Robert Begone.

Paul Mouse looked puzzled. "I felt like I could fly but there was a force inside of me that held me back."

Henry Right spun his wheelchair around in circles. "Next time I leave this chair for good."

As the people dispersed Nurse Steal announced, "Tomorrow at the same time for your second lesson." She then went over to Harold, who was standing by the window and gazing at the sky. "That was very good, Harold," she said.

Turning to face her, and to the surprise of Nurse Steal, there were tears in his eyes. "Need hope. No hope, no fly," he said despondently.

Nurse Steal hugged him. "I hope," she said softly. "And they will hope. You must give them time. They have been so long without it."

******

Martha Dearheart, Rose Merrywood, Grace Brethren, and Betty Frost were at their table. "Snapdragons around the edge of the garden would be nice," Betty Frost said.

"And a row of baby's-breath and some love-lies-bleeding," Rose Merrywood said.

"We will have to also have some bright red mums," Grace Brethren said.

Martha Dearheart was listening to the conversation and

rubbing her pearl pin. "Why Martha, I haven't seen you wear your pin in a while," Rose Merrywood said.

"Not wearing it makes me appreciate it more," Martha Dearheart answered after a pause.

Grace Brethren gave her a surprised look.

The buzzer to the door went off. "Attack, attack," George Early called as Nurse Sly, not in uniform, hurried through the dayroom and went to Mr. Dry's office.

Mr. Dry was surprised to see Nurse Sly and more surprised when she told him she was quitting for a better paying job. Nurse Sly went back to the dayroom and said in a low subdued voice to the residents, "I want you all to know I care deeply for you, but I have resigned." She hurried outside, holding back her tears until she was in her car.

"I take it she has had enough," Mr. Fist said to the group.

"Can't blame her," Robert Begone said, noticing he had only one shoe on.

"I don't know who could stand working around a bunch of old goats anyway," Paul Mouse said.

Jake Lost turned his hearing aid off and said nothing.

Mr. Dry rubbed his head. In the past three years, six nurses had quit, and he had lost count of the number of aides who had come and gone. He needed at least three registered nurses, but now there was only Nurse Steal. It was hard to find people who were dedicated enough to work for the low pay nursing homes paid. "Dear God," Mr. Dry beseeched.

Harold heard a noise like a lawn mower. Other people also heard the noise and headed down the hall to the window. Outside, a man was tilling about a twenty yard by twenty yard section of ground for the garden. "We can have cut flowers everywhere," Betty Frost said. "I'm allergic to flowers," George Early said.

"Tough," Grace Brethren said.

"If we grow rhubarb, we can make wine," George Early said to Henry Right.

"I'm going to fly out of here. My drinking days are over," Henry Right said with no doubt in his voice.

"If we learn how to fly, life will have been worth it," George Early said.

While the people were in the wing several men carried real plants into the dayroom and removed the plastic ones.

Mr. Dry felt pleased. Looking back over the past few years he wondered how he could have become so engrossed with the bottom line. "I have missed so much about humanity," he told himself. "I will never do it again. It has only harmed me."

With the majority of the residents watching the garden being tilled, Robert Begone dashed toward the front door. The buzzer sounded. "Robert, you cheated," Mr. Fist hollered.

By the time the aides caught up with Robert Begone, he was in the middle of the parking lot, leaning up against a car, with a Cheshire cat smile on his face.

Mr. Fist was in the dayroom when Robert Begone was brought back in. "You have the new record," Mr. Fist grumbled, but added, "You won't hold it for long."

Paul Mouse and Jake Lost came over and Paul Mouse handed Mr. Fist another page out of the *Playboy*. "It's not as good as flying, but it beats *Outdoor Life*," Paul Mouse said.

When the garden was tilled the ladies went back to their table. "It is like a dream," Grace Brethren said.

"When we learn how to fly we can sit in the trees and look at all the beautiful flowers," Rose Merrywood said.

Grace Brethren shook her head in disbelief but did not say anything.

To the ladies surprise and aide wheeled the new lady with her Raggedy Ann doll to the table. "Hello," Rose Merrywood said.

"God blesses you," Grace Brethren said.

"What an adorable child," Martha Dearheart said.

The lady rocked the Raggedy Ann doll gently in her arms.

"She is so well behaved," Rose Merrywood said.

"None of my children were ever quiet," Betty Frost said.

"I am alone," the lady said more to herself than the others.

"We have each other," Grace Brethren said soothingly.

"And Harold," Rose Merrywood said. "We have hope if we

can find it."

"What is your name?" Martha Dearheart asked.

The lady did not answer.

Grace Brethren noticed the real plants in the corners of the dayroom - pointing at them all the ladies sighed in unison - there was life.

Harold was thoroughly enjoying the spectacle of the birds splashing in the birdbath.

There were blue jays, big and cocky, bullies of the bird world. There were sparrows, paranoid of the slightest movement, like the small of all life. There were robins, bouncy and happy as if life had no problems. Harold did not know one bird from the other, they were all merely birds.

Nurse Steal joined Harold and felt his joy at the birds. She also laughed at the antics of the various birds. After a while, Harold started for the dining room and lunch. Nurse Steal was about to turn around when a small brown bird with red eyes landed on the birdbath. The bird's eyes seemed to bore into Nurse Steal's most secret thoughts. The other birds scattered. The bird drank slowly, took a quick bath, and then perched on the edge of the bird bath it sang, "Fa, La, La."

"Fa, La, La," Nurse Steal sang back.

"Fa, La, La," the bird sang.

Nurse Steal shut her eyes, spreading her arms she flapped them slowly, swaying with the song from the little bird. Suddenly, as though pushed by a wind, she felt like she was flying over the earth. She could see towns and cities, rivers, lakes and trees, gardens and yards, children playing and people working. She could feel in her mind the freedom of flight and the joy of leaving the world behind. Nurse Steal opened her eyes and stopped flapping her arms. To her fright, she was farther from the window than she had been. "My God," she gasped.

Martha Dearheart could not remember when she had eaten such a good lunch at Rest View. They had turkey, sweet potatoes, salad, and banana pudding. Now, resting in bed, she swore she would never again take off the pearl pin. It would go with her wherever she went. As she was about to doze off, the wail of an ambulance shook her back to reality as it stopped at Rest View.

Each resident in their own separate way tried to cope with the cry of the ambulance. They were torn between leaving their rooms or staying in their rooms and avoiding the dreadful reality.

After the ambulance departed, the residents slowly came out of their rooms. Mr. Fist, Robert Begone, and Jake Lost were by the magazine rack waiting nervously for Paul Mouse.

Nurse Steal approached them. She tried to smile but could not. She wanted to cry but could not. "Paul Mouse had a massive stroke and has died," she told the men tenderly.

The three men did not say anything but hung their heads.

"I wonder if he left his *Playboy*," Robert Begone asked after a few minutes of silence.

"I doubt it," Mr. Fist said.

"I'm sad," Robert Begone said.

"Me too," Jake Lost said and started crying.

The three men, avoiding each other's gaze, let the tears flow silently down their faces. After a few minutes, Mr. Fist yelled, "Bonsai," and ran as fast as he could toward the door.

"No you don't," Robert Begone called, starting after him.

Both men reached the door at the same time and pushed each other trying to be the first through. The alarm sounded. "Dive, dive," George Early yelled.

Harold started flapping his arms and skipping around the dayroom. Two aides ran from the hall and crashed into Harold and all three sprawled on the floor.

The aides scrambled to their feet leaving Harold, still flapping his arms, sitting on the floor and yelling, "Paul angel, Paul fly."

When the aides caught up with Mr. Fist and Robert Begone, they were neck and neck at the far side of the parking lot. "The world record is a tie," Robert Begone puffed.

Mr. Fist was about to argue, but looking at Robert Begone's feet he said, "You can have the shoeless record and give me the record for having shoes on."

The men gravely shook hands.

Back inside, Mr. Fist announced, "Even."

The ladies at the table applauded sadly and Harold flapped his way down the hall.

Nurse Steal, looking at the two old men with their tears dried on their faces, choked back a tear and felt deeply touched by the pain and joy of it all.

******

Nurse Steal placed everything Paul Mouse had owned into one cardboard box. The janitor would come in and disinfect and re-wax the floor. The sheets would be changed and everything made ready for another person.

Nurse Steal took Paul Mouse's possessions to a storage room, labeled them with a black grease pencil and shut the door, entombing the socks, underwear, several pairs of pants, and a photograph of a young woman sitting by a stream. There was no name on the back of the photograph.

******

Now that Nurse Sly had quit, Nurse Steal and Hazel volunteered to do extra hours until another nurse was hired. Nurse Steal was not really bothered because at Rest View she felt needed, where at home she felt nothing. She told Mr. Dry, "Sixteen hours here is like sixteen hours anyplace, it is only time."

After dinner Hazel announced that there would be bingo.

"I'm not playing," Mr. Fist said. "I am in mourning."

"I don't think anybody wants to play this evening," Martha Dearheart said.

Hazel nodded her head in understanding. Nurse Steal followed the residents down the hall.

Martha Dearheart put on her nightgown although it would not be dark for an hour. Tomorrow she was giving the list of seeds the residents wanted for the garden to Nurse Steal. She took the pearl pin off of her dress, put it on her nightgown, and got into bed. She had a passing thought of Paul Mouse, but pushed it from her mind. Taking a deep breath, she shut her eyes, "You may take me when you want," she prayed.

Rose Merrywood was waiting for Nurse Steal to come and

help her undress for bed. She flapped her arms and put a vision in her head of a wren flying through a field of sunflowers.

Grace Brethren picked up her Bible. Lowering her head, she prayed. "Paul Mouse. Do not fear, we are all sinners, but I know you were good of heart and God will embrace you."

Jake Lost turned off his hearing aid and let his head fall back on the pillow. "Oh Paul, I would rather have died before you. I do not want to be last. Please? Don't let me be last."

Robert Begone looked at the foot of his bed and then at his feet. He was wearing one brown shoe and one black shoe, but at the end of his bed were two black shoes, and two brown shoes. He was confused for a moment but then he smiled. "Paul Mouse must have left them to me in his will. I will take good care of them."

Mr. Fist wished he was sitting in a boat in the middle of a lake. He didn't care if he was fishing, he only wanted to sit in a boat in the middle of a lake and hear the sound of the water as it touched the boat. There had always been something peaceful to him in the sound. Mr. Fist flapped his arms several times and then let them fall heavily to his sides. "We spend our time dreaming. Dreaming for a family, dreaming we will get money, dreaming we will have a nice home, a car, always dreaming. And when we reach a dream, we dream for something else. I think dreams are put in front of us to make us want to live. Paul, dear Paul, I hope you know I loved you."

Mr. Fist changed into his pajamas and turned his covers down. To his surprise the *Playboy* was under his pillow, but it brought him no joy.

Harold put his tennis shoes under his bed and took off his bib overalls. He folded them neatly and laid them over the back of his chair. He got down on his knees and prayed. "I must teach fly. Paul now angel. Harold angel. Harold fly with Paul."

When Harold felt all the residents were sleeping he got out of bed. Nurse Steal had gone home leaving Hazel with instructions to call her if anything happened. Harold tip-toed to the window, "Fa, La, La," he sang softly.

A few moments later a bird sang back. "Fa, La, La."

Harold shut his eyes and started flapping his arms.

The night sky was radiant as Harold flew. But even though the stars were bright, Harold's heart was troubled. He had a deep foreboding he might not be able to teach hope. There was no sense of freedom that filled his mind, no sense of direction, only the flight of the lost seeking what cannot be found.

When Harold was back he went to Rose Merrywood. Harold held her hand gently. "Tell me about the stars," Rose Merrywood said.

"Harold need help teach hope," Harold begged. "Harold not know how."

"No, Harold, you in your simple way can truly know hope. That is why you can fly and we can only dream about flying, the rest of us made our lives too complicated," Rose Merrywood said.

"Need help," Harold begged.

"Just be yourself," Rose Merrywood said.

"Harold love all people," Harold said.

"I know, but love is not hope."

Harold went back to his room. "Fa, La, La," the bird sang outside, but Harold ignored it.

Chapter Nine

Mr. Dry was at home relaxing in his easy chair. The children were in bed and his wife was sitting of the sofa reading a magazine. "I think I have figured out the main problem with our old folks system," he said to his wife. "We only think about the physical side of being old. We don't put enough emphasis on making the people feel useful to society. We separate them and we put them in homes where the rest of the world forgets about them. We have made being old a sin and in doing so we have made the old and wise people of our country lonely."

"You can't change the system," his wife said pragmatically.

"I might not be able to, but I should try. Growing old should not make one feel as though they have done something wrong," Mr. Dry said.

******

Nurse Steal was in her nightgown by the open window. The curtains did not move in the windless night. She could hear crickets. She tried not to think about Paul Mouse, but she could not get the thought of him out of her mind. She wondered what his life had been like. She wondered if he had been in a war. How many women had he loved? She wondered if he had ever fulfilled one of his dreams or if life had led him along and never let him know he had been a special part, unique in his own way upon the face of the earth. After a while she did not think about Paul Mouse. Working around death, she knew one must not ponder death. She started to think about Harold. She smiled ironically over the fact she had even gone to the extent of spying on Harold to see if he could fly. "God," she said. "I must be so lonely I think we can fly. How many straws can one search for?"

Shutting the window she pictured Harold while he was giving his first flying class. She shook her head sadly and wondered why man struggled so to survive and find meaning in life when in most instances life was just a riddle that had no answer, or at the very least, an answer that changed while the riddle stayed the same.

Turning off the light, she wished there was somebody in bed with her, somebody with whom to share a few moments of warmth. "Fa, La, La," drifted into the room. Nurse Steal jumped out of bed, turned the light back on, and opened the window. "Fa, La, La," sang a small brown bird with a splash of blue on his chest.

"Don't tease me," she said. "Go away, go away and leave me alone. I am too old to dream."

But the bird did not stop singing. "Fa, La, La, Fa, La, La."

"I don't want to believe," Nurse Steal pleaded. "Life is better without hopes and dreams. Don't you understand?"

Nurse Steal's words seemed to make the bird sad. It started to fly away, but stopped and sang, "Fa, La, La," once more before disappearing into the dark. "Oh Harold, I hope you do not lose faith," Nurse Steal said.

******

The residents were all gathered for their flying lesson - all except Grace Brethren and the new lady, but Harold had not shown up. He had also not been at breakfast. Nurse Steal had gone to check on him during breakfast and found him looking at the birdbath. "Are you ok?" she asked.

114

"Harold need think," he replied seriously.

Nurse Steal left him alone and went back to the dining room.

Waiting for Harold Rose Merrywood was flapping her arms up and down slowly as though testing for the wind. The other residents were excited.

Harold entered the dayroom from the east wing. Whatever had been bothering him seemed to have passed, as he was smiling expansively. He flapped his arms several times and sang loudly, "Fa, La, La."

"Fa, La, La," everybody sang back.

Harold started flapping around the room and all the residents flapped their arms. Nurse Steal joined in.

Mr. Dry was watching from his doorway. "Harold, you poor man. After spending all your life in some institution you probably think you really can fly," he said.

After shutting the door, Mr. Dry looked out the window at the bright summer day, whistled and flapped his arms several times.

Harold stopped flapping his arms and the residents followed suit. His expression changed and everyone could feel a deep sadness radiating from him. It was a sadness that seemed to cling to the marrow of his bones. "When Harold young nobody play with Harold," Harold said. "Everybody laugh. Harold never have parents. Harold all alone. But Harold learn dream. Harold learn smile. Harold learn be good boy. Harold not like being alone, but Harold learn hope. Harold learn bird's friends. Little bird come to Harold and teach fly. Please, all people here Harold's friends. Harold teach fly. Must hope. Not old, not young, just hope. Must hope."

Harold shut his eyes and sang in a child's voice, "Go to sleep little one, all the world is sleeping, go to dreams, to dreams, all the world is dreaming, learn to love, learn to be, learn to dance with the heavens, soon you fly, soon you fly, and your heart will learn singing."

Harold turned away from the people and headed for his room, while perched unnoticed on the windowsill of the dayroom, looking in, a small brown bird with mysterious red eyes sang, "Fa, La, La," before flying away.

After a long moment of silence, Rose Merrywood proclaimed, "I will learn how to hope."

"Me too," Mr. Fist said.

"For Paul Mouse," Jake Lost said.

Martha Dearheart touched her pearl pin.

Henry Right started flapping his arms. "We can do it. I am telling you we can do it."

As if on cue, all the residents started flapping their arms. Nurse Steal did not have the heart to stop them.

******

The next morning after breakfast aides pushed Rose Merrywood, Bertha Shields and Randolph, Betty Frost and Gloria Sane to the garden. Martha Dearheart helped Grace Brethren. Mr. Fist, Robert Begone, and Jake Lost were examining the freshly tilled dirt. Nurse Steal and Hazel came out each with a shovel and a rake.

"This is so exciting," Rose Merrywood said to Betty Frost.

People who did not want to go outside sat by the wing window and watched. The lady and her Raggedy Ann doll were in her room gazing at the wall.

"I do hope I live long enough to see things growing," Betty Frost said.

"Where is Wilma Happy?" Gloria Sane asked.

"Wilma is not feeling well," Nurse Steal answered.

"Mr. Fist, Robert Begone, and Jake Lost have volunteered to do the planting under our guidance," Nurse Steal announced.

The ladies smiled at the men.

"It has been decided that we will plant radishes in the first row," Martha Dearheart announced, handing a package of seeds to Mr. Fist.

Mr. Fist made a shallow furrow and Robert Begone, wearing only one shoe, followed, spacing the seeds carefully. Jake Lost covered the furrow. When they were done, Mr. Fist stuck the seed package on a stick and stuck it at the end of the row.

"Lettuce," Martha Dearheart announced.

As the men were planting the lettuce, Harold came outside and skipped around the garden. "We will need a scarecrow to keep all the birds away from the seeds," Bertha Shields said.

Harold hurried back into Rest View and returned quickly with a pair of his bib overalls. He then flapped down to the trees and came back with a big stick. He stuck the stick in the ground and draped his overalls over it. "That is a lovely scarecrow," Bertha Shields said just as two birds flew over and landed on the scarecrow.

"Let them eat," Henry Right said. "They can't eat it all."

"I agree," Rose Merrywood said. "Besides, when we learn how to fly we can eat some ourselves."

"When we learn how to fly I am going to fly to Florida for the winter," Betty Frost said.

Hazel smiled at Nurse Steal.

"Now mums," Martha Dearheart said.

"Don't get the seeds too close together," Mr. Fist told Robert Begone.

"You just dig the furrow and mind your own business," Robert Begone said.

"We want corn next," Henry Right said.

After the corn was planted Nurse Steal said, "That is enough for today, tomorrow you can plant more. I don't want you all getting too tired before Harold's flying class."

"First we must pray over the garden," Grace Brethren said.

"Do we have to?" Henry Right protested.

"Let her pray. A little prayer never hurt anybody as long as it does not go on forever," George Early said.

"Dear Lord," Grace Brethren began. "As you take all life in your hands, bless our tiny garden, let the seeds grow to their fulfillment, and let us feast from thy bounty. Amen."

"Amen," the people responded.

"How lovely," Hazel said.

It was decided that after all the excitement Harold would not give his flying class until after lunch. Harold stopped at the door to the room of the lady and her Raggedy Ann doll. She was gazing at the bare wall. He went inside and looked at the wall trying to see what the lady was seeing. He tilted his head sideways, first to the left and then to the right. He put his nose almost on the wall, and confused he turned back toward the lady. "I see the ocean, and sailing out over the ocean I see seagulls and a great albatross with a fish in his mouth. On a white beach there are a man and a woman holding hands while walking. They are in love," the lady said.

Harold looked at the wall once again. "I see seagulls," he said.

"My name is Letha Johnston," the lady said.

"Me Harold. Harold good boy."

The dining room was full when Harold pushed Letha Johnston and the Raggedy Ann doll in. Stopping in front of everybody Harold announced, "Letha likes seagulls."

"I am Letha Johnston and this is my baby Carrie, I hope you will all grow to like me and Carrie," Letha said in a quiet shy voice.

"Everybody say hello to Letha," Hazel said.

"Hello, Letha," all the people responded.

Harold pushed Letha close to the other ladies.

Bertha Shields said to Letha, "I am glad to know your name. Nobody else around here has a baby and I need somebody to talk to who knows what it is like."

Letha smiled.

"Will you be taking flying lessons?" Betty Frost asked Letha.

"I think I am too old," Letha Johnston said.

"Harold told me even old birds fly," Rose Merrywood said.

"Does Randolph take flying lessons?" Letha Johnston asked Bertha Shields.

"Randolph loves them."

"Then Carrie and I will take them also," Letha Johnston said.

Henry Right wheeled over to Harold and whispered to him. "Harold, I want a private lesson. I haven't told anyone, but I flew over an inch."

Harold thought seriously for a moment. "Tonight," he

whispered back. "Harold teach private."

Henry Right wheeled back over to George Early.

"After lunch there will be a rest break for an hour and then Harold will give his lesson," Hazel announced.

"For all the rest we get you'd think we would be growing younger and not older," Mr. Fist grumped.

Nurse Steal did her paperwork and then made her rounds. They still had not found a replacement for Nurse Sly and Nurse Steal was beginning to wonder if they ever would. Grace Brethren was thinking about the garden. Nurse Steal went into the room. "Life is such a strange thing," Grace Brethren said. "We are all like a garden. All of us are nothing when we are born, then we get planted with seeds of every type imaginable. Seeds that grow to be flowers and vegetables and seeds that grow to be weeds. It is so easy in life to become a weed."

"It is easier to become a weed," Nurse Steal said.

"I wonder if God really does listen to us," Grace Brethren said, shocking Nurse Steal. "You look around and see all the beautiful things, but then you look around and you see all the bad and ugly things. At times it seems God does not really care. Life so random and haphazard."

"I don't know," Nurse Steal sighed. "I remember when I was a little girl I used to get down on my knees every night before bed and pray. I prayed I would grow up to be a nurse. But one day I stopped praying. I stopped praying for a better world, everything just seems to get worse. Nothing seems to get better. We just hang on from day to day and before long we no longer look to the future for anything but another day. We plod along and ignore everything that is going on around us, as if by ignoring, all the bad will go away."

"You are old before your time," Grace Brethren said.

"I know," Nurse Steal agreed.

"I don't think I will see the garden grow," Grace Brethren said.

"Yes you will," Nurse Steal said.

"No, I don't think so," Grace Brethren said. "But it does not make me sad."

"I am sure you will go to heaven," Nurse Steal said. "You have led a very pious life."

"There has been more than one thorn in my life," Grace Brethren said. "More than anybody but me knows."

"Why don't you take flying lessons?" Nurse Steal asked.

"If God would have wanted us to fly, we would fly," Grace Brethren replied, but with a distant smile.

"Grace, there is more to it than that," Nurse Steal said.

******

Hazel was moving things around in the dayroom for Harold's flying lesson, and for the first time in a long time Nurse Steal noticed how young and pretty Hazel was. It seemed to strike her like a hammer blow, and she felt how quickly her own life was racing by. "They really like these lessons," Nurse Steal said to Hazel.

"We all live on dreams of air," Hazel said.

"All except Harold, he lives on dreams of hope."

"Fa, La, La," Hazel sang.

Nurse Steal flapped her arms several times, but she suddenly felt weak and she hurried to the nurses' station to sit down. I need some rest, she thought, finding it difficult to catch her breath.

Wilma Happy was still not feeling well and her and Grace Brethren were the only people not gathered for the flying lesson. Harold skipped into the dayroom flapping his arms and singing, "Fa, La, La."

"Our salvation," Mr. Fist hollered.

Harold stopped in front of the group and flapped his arms slowly. All the residents followed his cadence. Nurse Steal, although feeling ill, flapped her arms. Even Hazel joined in. Mr. Fist was flapping his arms faster than anybody else and standing on his tiptoes hoping to get an edge on the competition. Henry Right flapped his arms thinking any minute he would soar into the sky. Rose Merrywood flapped her arms with her eyes closed wishing she could gain hope. Martha Dearheart flapped her arms more not to discourage any of the group who believed in such foolishness. While Bertha Shields, Letha, Betty Frost and Gloria Sane flapped their arms merely because it was fun.

Robert Begone said to Mr. Fist, who was beginning to turn red. "You know, if I could learn how to fly, I wouldn't have to worry about my shoes."

Harold stopped flapping his arms and motioned for the others to stop. Mr. Fist beat his arms a few more times and fell backwards into a chair, breathing heavily.

Harold sang, "Fa, La, La," and then said, "Each person tell why hope," and pointed first at Rose Merrywood.

Rose Merrywood said in a low, distant voice, "I don't think I can hope, Harold. I keep trying, but nothing happens."

"What can we hope for Harold? A few more years stuck in a wheelchair?" Betty Frost asked.

"They have taken hope away from us," George Early said. "Hope is somewhere beyond these walls."

Harold looked at Martha Dearheart. Martha tried to think of something to say, but in truth all she hoped for was the return of her garnet pin. "I can't help you, Harold," she finally said despondently.

Mr. Fist jumped to his feet. "I hope to die free," he shouted.

"Me too," Robert Begone said.

"Only the young can hope," George Early said.

"We want to hope," Betty Frost said. "But I suppose we spend our time going from one useless dream to another. Dreams we know that will never be fulfilled, dreams that in truth only take us farther and farther away from the truth."

"What is truth?" Harold questioned.

"The truth is we are useless," Rose Merrywood said, bowing her head.

The room grew silent as though a dense fog of remorse had sifted under the doors and engulfed everyone. Harold looked at Nurse Steal and then at Randolph. He looked at his tennis shoes, which were untied, and he looked out the window. Pointing at the window, he said, "Hope not sky. Hope not young, hope here, hope friends. Must hope."

Nurse Steal sang, "Fa, La, La."

"Please learn," Harold begged.

"Fa, La, La," Nurse Steal sang again.

"We still want to take flying lessons, Harold, even if we cannot hope," Rose Merrywood said.

"I know," Harold said. "Harold must learn to be better teacher."

"We will learn how to fly," Mr. Fist said.

Everyone nodded their heads.

Rose Merrywood wheeled herself into Wilma Happy's room. Wilma Happy was in bed looking very pale. The sunlight streaming into the room made it seem as though Wilma was floating with the dust particles. "Are you feeling better?" Rose Merrywood asked.

"Did you fly?" Wilma Happy asked.

"No, but I tried."

"Dust floating in the air has always amazed me," Wilma Happy said. "It seems as if every tiny little particle is a life, a life with no direction, only being pushed and pulled by the soft breezes to where it finally settles where it never planned."

"I've never thought about it," Rose Merrywood said. "In fact, I have never thought much about life. Life to me was being married and having children and teaching."

"You have had a good life," Wilma Happy said.

"Is it impossible for us to hope again?" Rose Merrywood asked.

"I don't know," Wilma Happy answered. "But if we were strong enough, I don't see why not."

Martha Dearheart was observing the birdbath when Harold joined her. "Harold good boy," Harold said.

"Better than most of us," Martha Dearheart said.

"Harold not give up teach fly," Harold said.

"Good, we need you," Martha Dearheart said.

Two blue jays landed on the birdbath, flopped around in the water and flew off.

Harold and Martha Dearheart laughed.

Martha Dearheart touched the pearl pin on her collar and felt a deep pang of grief spread through her heart. She patted

Harold tenderly on the shoulder and went to the dayroom. Hazel was sorting through boxes of crayons, getting all the colors back together. Martha Dearheart went over to her. "Were you ever in love so deeply nothing else in the world seemed to matter?" Hazel asked.

"I loved my husband more than my life," Martha Dearheart said.

"I don't think people fall in love like they used to," Hazel said. "We do not trust and can only offer the corner of our hearts, if we are brave enough even for that."

"I still love my husband," Martha Dearheart said.

"I think the flying lessons might have been a mistake," Hazel said.

"I don't think so. At least they are making us look at the truth," Martha Dearheart said.

"The truth hurts," Hazel said.

"Maybe hope only comes after great pain," Martha Dearheart said.

Hazel put her face in her hands and started to cry. "At times I am so afraid of the future," she sobbed.

Martha Dearheart hugged Hazel. "Fear is with us our entire lives," she soothed.

"Why?" Hazel cried.

"If man knew, why, we would not have wars or greed."

Hazel wiped her eyes. "Maybe love isn't the answer," she said.

"Maybe it never was," Martha Dearheart said. "Maybe friends are the answer."

******

Harold listened intently from his bed. By now everybody should be asleep. He looked down the hall and did not see Hazel at the nurses' station and darted to Henry Right's room. Henry Right's wheelchair was at the foot of his bed. "I'm glad you came," he said to Harold. "I hope, with all my heart I hope."

Harold opened Henry Right's window as far as he could. Within a few minutes both he and Henry Right heard, "Fa, La,

La," and they started to flap their arms.

Harold shut his eyes and Henry Right did also.

Henry Right felt air rushing over his arms.

"What are you two doing?" Hazel's voice cut through the room.

Henry Right opened his eyes and lowered his arms. "Teach fly," Harold said timidly.

"You two are supposed to be in bed. Flying lessons are during the day," Hazel scolded.

"We were flying," Henry Right said excitedly. "I could see Rest View from the air. It was wonderful."

"Hazel fly," Harold said.

"You go to your room, Harold. And Henry you get back into bed," Hazel ordered.

"But we flew," Henry Right protested.

Harold headed toward his room.

"There has always been somebody who stood in the way of all great scientific breakthroughs," Henry Right told Hazel.

"Your scientific breakthroughs can happen during the day," Hazel said.

Harold got into bed and giggled. "Harold fly and Henry fly, Harold good teacher."

Back at the nurses' station, Hazel wondered why she had been so severe with Harold and Henry Right. "People should be able to fly. I hope by the time I am old man has learned how to fly," she muttered angrily at herself.

Chapter Ten

Mr. Dry was in his office and deeply troubled. Not one nurse had applied for the opening. He knew Nurse Steal and Hazel could not take the extra work for much longer. If there were no applications soon he would have to hire a temporary and temporaries more often than not were not reliable. He glanced at a report from Nurse Steal on the flying lessons. 'As to this date no one has been able to fly,' Nurse Steal wrote. Mr. Dry smiled. Other paperwork informed him medication costs were rising, cleaning supplies were more expensive, and the cost of food was skyrocketing. Also, the ambulance service wanted to charge more. There was a knock on the door. There were three men all in their thirties and dressed in suits and ties. "We are state inspectors," one of the men said. "We wanted you to know we are here."

The Rest View Incorporation hired private inspectors to inspect all of their facilities. Because rest homes are inspected by both state and federal agencies Rest View tried their best to always be in compliance.

"If you need any help you know where I am," Mr. Dry said with a sense of foreboding.

******

Nurse Steal smiled as the last row of seeds was covered and said, "Somebody be sure to go by Wilma Happy's room and tell her the garden is all planted."

"I will," Rose Merrywood said

"All right, everybody back inside," Nurse Steal said. "Today after lunch Hazel has a surprise for us. She hasn't told me what it is, but she let me know everyone will enjoy it."

"Maybe she is going to do a table dance," Robert Begone said.

"That would be nice," Mr. Fist said.

"What?" Jake Lost hollered.

"Dance," Robert Begone hollered back.

"I don't dance," Jake Lost said.

Grace Brethren examined the garden. When you are blooming and filled with life I will be gone, she thought.

While the residents filed back inside, the three inspectors watched them intently.

It did not take long for the residents to discover the three men were inspectors and they tried their best to avoid them. During lunch, the three men toured the dining room, talking secretly between themselves.

After lunch, Hazel brought out a cart holding a large bowl of popcorn. "Popcorn," Mr. Fist said happily.

"Carrie loves popcorn," Letha Johnston said.

"You can have Randolph's," Bertha Shields said. "It bothers his stomach and makes him grumpy."

"Birds love popcorn," Harold said.

"The birds better not like our garden," Robert Begone said.

Harold frowned but said nothing.

After the popcorn was gone Nurse Steal announced, "Flying lessons in an hour and a half."

"And now we must rest," Mr. Fist butted in.

"Twenty hours a day," Rose Merrywood said.

"And while you rest, think about flying," Hazel said.

"Hazel take lessons?" Harold asked.

"Yes, today I think I will," Hazel said.

Nurse Steal went to see Wilma Happy. "I will make the flying lesson today," Wilma Happy said.

Back in the dayroom, Nurse Steal watched the three inspectors. They were at the end of the hall looking at the birdbath. She wondered why they never asked her any questions about the mental well being of the residents. All they were interested in was sanitation and records. There was never anything about the true purpose of the home - people.

Nurse Steal went to see Harold. "You believe fly?" Harold asked like a child that needed encouragement.

"I try," she said.

Harold hugged her.

Back in the dayroom Hazel said to Nurse Steal, "You look tired."

"I have not had much energy lately," Nurse Steal said. "I feel weak."

"You should tell Mr. Dry. You are working yourself too hard."

"The people need me. They are more important," Nurse Steal said.

Harold was standing stoically in front of the people gathered for his flying lesson. Once again Grace Brethren was in her room. Robert Begone had discovered he was not wearing any shoes and only one sock. "Now people are even stealing my socks," he said to Mr. Fist.

"It's only natural," Mr. Fist said. "Small crimes normally lead to larger more brazen crimes."

Jake Lost was fiddling with his hearing aid, but instead of turning it up, he was turning it down.

Henry Right had his arms straight out waiting for Harold to tell them to start flapping them. "Today you will see," he told George Early.

"We want to fly," Mr. Fist hollered.

Harold started flapping his arms and all the residents joined in. Just then the three inspectors came out of the west wing and observed the group.

Harold skipped around the people. "Fa, La, La," he sang.

"Fa, La, La," they chorused back.

Mr. Fist once again beat his arms twice as fast as the others. Henry Right was so intense his face started to turn red. Rose Merrywood closed her eyes and pictured a wren in her mind. George Early scoffed at Henry Right, "Well fly, you idiot."

Hazel flapped her arms while watching Nurse Steal carefully. She was worried about her.

By now Mr. Fist was beating his arms so furiously he fell back into his chair. Jake Lost hollered, "You ran out of runway."

Harold sensed they were getting tired and he stopped. "Better," he said.

"I hope so," Rose Merrywood said. "All this practice has to be doing something."

"You're still here," George Early said to Henry Right.

"It's your fault," Henry Right said. "You don't try hard enough."

"I feel like quitting," George Early said.

"You can't quit," Martha Dearheart said.

"Please, no quit," Harold pleaded.

"Don't listen to George Early," Bertha Shields said to Randolph.

"Don't lose hope over us," Mr. Fist said to Harold.

"To break out of here, a tunnel or a car is still our best bet," Robert Begone said.

Harold's shoulders slumped and he started toward his room.

"I was only kidding," George Early apologized.

Harold tried to smile but he was troubled.

"It's a good thing you were only kidding," Mr. Fist warned George Early.

"We all fly tomorrow," Harold said.

"We will all fly tomorrow," Rose Merrywood repeated.

"No doubt," Henry Right said to George Early, then whispered, "I know you really want to quit."

"What did everybody say?" Jake Lost asked Mr. Fist.

"They are going to sell all your shoes," Mr. Fist said.

"Selling stolen property is against the law," Jake Lost said.

Bertha Shields and Randolph were sitting by Letha Johnston and Carrie. "It is a good thing we have babies," Bertha Shields said.

"Yes it is, at least we have a purpose," Letha Johnston said.

Harold was watching the birdbath, but the four sparrows that were bathing did not make him smile.

Nurse Steal approached him. "Harold wants to be alone. Harold confused on teaching."

Nurse Steal hugged him. "You will work it out," she said.

Mr. Dry escorted the three inspectors to the front door. Something is not good. I can tell by Mr. Dry's face Hazel thought.

Everyone was surprised, when after supper, Mr. Dry came to the dining room. "I really don't know how to tell you what I have to say, but first let me tell you I am truly sorry. The inspectors were here today and I must inform you, you cannot have a garden."

"Communist," Mr. Fist hollered.

"They say it is for your well being," Mr. Dry went on. "We can only serve FDA inspected food."

"How about growing flowers?" Rose Merrywood asked.

Mr. Dry shook his head.

Martha Dearheart was devastated.

Grace Brethren covered her mouth with her hand.

"You also can no longer have flying lessons. Harold is not a state-licensed physical therapist."

Nurse Steal was aghast. Harold ran from the room.

Rose Merrywood sobbed.

"Poor Harold," Wilma Happy said.

"Physical therapists can't teach us how to fly," Mr. Fist argued.

"Why don't they just lock the door and throw away the key," Henry Right said. "Then they can really forget about us."

Mr. Dry went to his office knowing he was not even a clog in the wheel.

Harold had thumb in his mouth when three sparrows landed in the redbud tree. "Go away," Harold ordered, waving his arms angrily. "Harold no like birds."

The birds flew away.

Nurse Steal entered the room. Harold turned but he did not look at her. Nurse Steal had never seen him so serious. "Alone," Harold said. "Leave alone."

"Oh, Harold, you have to understand. Nobody is in control anymore, we are all governed by rules most of us don't have any power over."

"Harold no care. Harold no teach fly anymore."

"Many people care, Harold. We really do."

"No more fly. No more hope. People not care about us."

"You will fly again, Harold. It will take time, but you will fly again," Nurse Steal said.

"No fly, no fly."

"What about me?" Nurse Steal asked.

"Harold sad," he said, turning his back to her.

Nurse Steal left the room feeling empty. Harold shooed two more birds away.

Martha Dearheart felt cheated - cheated by the fact that life would once again go on as usual. She knew the residents would in time forget the garden. They would also forget the flying lessons. Thinking about the flying lessons Martha Dearheart smiled. They had been fun and foolish. But having something foolish was, in itself, a stand against the system - a statement that one could still laugh and have fun.

"I never flew," Henry Right told himself. "I only dreamed I flew, dreamed like I have dreamed most of my life away. Never really seeing what things are like, but seeing them the way I wanted to see them. But it would have been grand to fly. It would have been very grand."

Robert Begone was in his room, puzzled. He now had four pair of shoes under his bed.

Mr. Fist was in the middle of his room flapping his arms up and down furiously. "We could have done it with just a few more lessons. By God, I know we could have." He ran from his room and darted for the front door. He raced past George Early and Henry Right, who were playing checkers. No one was at the nurses' station. The buzzer sounded. When Mr. Fist reached the end of the parking lot, he could not believe he had not been stopped. Hurrying on he darted toward the trees behind Rest View.

All of the aides had been working and by the time they responded to the buzzer they did not find anybody outside. "Did anybody go out?" an aide asked George Early and Henry Right.

"Didn't see anybody," Henry Right said as pious as a monk.

"Me either," George Early replied.

Mr. Fist relaxed at the base of a tree. He could barely see the roof of Rest View. He breathed deeply. There was no smell of disinfectant, no odor of medicines. There was no sound of people, no grating of wheelchairs, or the clanking of walkers. He gazed at the sky through the gaps between the trees branches, an occasional cloud drifted peacefully through. Mr. Fist rested his head back against the trunk of the tree. "It's an all time record, with and without shoes," he smiled.

When supper was served it was discovered Mr. Fist was missing. George Early and Henry Right fessed up. "He escaped late this afternoon."

"You both were naughty," Rose Merrywood scolded George Early and Henry Right.

"Randolph does not lie," Bertha Shields said.

"Carrie does sometimes," Letha Johnston confessed.

Nurse Steal and an aide hurried outside, but stopped immediately. Mr. Fist was sitting on the front porch. "It was a lovely afternoon," he said. "I haven't bothered to think about what a day is really like in years. I forgot about wind and the sound of things and how it felt to be alone. We forget we are a creature of the earth."

"Why did you come back?" Nurse Steal asked tenderly.

"I have no place to go," he said quietly. "I realized this is my home."

When Mr. Fist entered the dining room, everyone applauded. "New record?" Robert Begone asked.

"No, we are still tied."

"I'll be damned," Robert Begone said.

"Me too," Mr. Fist said.

Hazel announced, "Bingo tonight."

"You wanted the same old routine," Henry Right said to George Early.

"I was wrong," George Early said.

"Carrie wants to play bingo," Letha Johnston said.

"She doesn't have a chance against Randolph," Bertha Shields warned her.

******

The person was in bed, their head propped up by a pillow. The dim light from the hall filtered into the room sending motionless shadows into the corners. The person's eyes scanned the shadows before gazing at one hand, palm up, resting on the covers. The garnet pin seemed to be filled with new life and promise - but it brought no joy.

******

Harold was in bed. From outside his window he heard, "Fa, La, La."

He did not get up.

The small brown bird with red eyes flew from the redbud tree and landed on the windowsill. "Fa, La, La," it called.

"Harold no fly, go away," he said to the bird.

"Fa, La, La," the bird beckoned.

"No come back," Harold ordered.

The bird started to sing, but stopped, and flew away.

******

Nurse Steal tidied up her apartment. She knew she needed rest but she did not feel sleepy. She could not stop thinking about Mr. Fist's statement, "I have no place to go." About to open the window she heard, "Fa, La, La," and opened the window. A small brown bird with red eyes flew into the room and landed on her table. The bird looked at Nurse Steal and flapped its wings several times.

"Who or what are you?" Nurse Steal asked feeling a kinship with the little bird.

"Fa, La, La," the bird sang.

"I am not the one. You are wasting your time. Don't you understand?" Nurse Steal said, but not knowing if she believed her words or not.

The bird flapped its wings again.

"No," Nurse Steal said, shaking her head, but added, "Are you friends with the little bird with a splash of blue?"

The bird flew and landed on Nurse Steal's shoulder and sang softly in her ear, "Fa, La, La."

"I can't help you," Nurse Steal said despondently. "Only Harold believes."

The little brown bird with the red eyes flew out the window.

Nurse Steal shut the window. "I am sorry. I am truly sorry," she said.

******

Mr. Dry was silent.

"What is it?" his wife asked.

"Nobody can fly," Mr. Dry said.

"Don't talk to me in riddles," his wife said.

"The inspectors have stopped the flying lessons and we have to take out the garden," Mr. Dry said.

"I figured as much," his wife said.

"It was worth a try. They enjoyed it while it lasted," Mr. Dry said.

"I hope it does not depress them," his wife said.

"I am going to appeal," Mr. Dry said.

His wife looked worried. "You could lose your job."

"It is better than losing my heart."

******

The residents watched as once again a man tilled the garden. He then scattered grass seed over the garden and hooked up a sprinkler to water in the seed. "Why don't you give us flying lessons on the sly?" Mr. Fist asked Harold.

"Harold no fly. Harold only walk," Harold said.

"One of us has to keep flying," Rose Merrywood said.

Harold shook his head.

"I guess I was wrong in thinking we could change our world," Martha Dearheart said.

"At least we gave it a shot," Henry Right said.

"We could have another meeting and come up with other things we want," Rose Merrywood said.

"There is no need," Martha Dearheart said. "They have sufficiently stuck us away to where we are not visible. People really don't care. What happens to us does not affect them."

"It's a terrible ending," Robert Begone said.

"It is," Rose Merrywood said. "What can we say? I am glad I am old. I am happy I cannot walk. I am overjoyed my joints hurt all the time and my fingers are twisted into knots."

"It is a good thing we have Nurse Steal and Hazel," Betty Frost said. "They care for us."

"We also have each other," Mr. Fist said.

"What?" Jake Lost asked, messing with his hearing aid.

"I wonder if one can love when they can't hear." Robert Begone asked.

"Love does not have to hear," Rose Merrywood said.

"I love you all," Mr. Fist said, heading toward his room.

"I love you," Robert Begone said to Mr. Fist's back.

"Love, love," Harold said and started to flap his arms, but caught himself and let his arms fall heavily to his sides.

"What?" Jake Lost asked again.

Rose Merrywood pushed her wheelchair over to Jake Lost and kissed him on the cheek.

"Oh, love," Jake Lost said, smiling.

******

Mr. Fist, Robert Begone, and Jake Lost were by the magazine rack talking secretively.

Henry Right and George Early were playing checkers. Harold, Bertha Shields and Randolph, Letha Johnston and Carrie were watching Mr. Rogers. Mr. Rogers was giving lessons on how to tie shoes. "Randolph is lucky," Bertha Shields said. "He does not need shoes."

Harold tied a loose bow. "Very good," Bertha Shields said.

"Harold trying to be good boy again," Harold said.

"I think Randolph and Carrie are getting old enough they could have a babysitter at times and you and I could do something on our own," Letha Johnston said to Bertha Shields.

"Harold baby sit," Harold said.

"I don't know if you could handle both of them," Letha Johnston said.

"Harold is good with children," Bertha Shields said.

Harold nodded his head.

"As long as you don't teach them how to fly," Letha Johnston said.

"No fly, no fly forever," Harold said.

Nurse Steal was in Mr. Dry's office. "I am terribly sorry about the inspectors stopping the flying lessons and the garden and I want you to know I am going to appeal the decision to the Board of Directors," Mr. Dry said.

Mr. Dry handed Nurse Steal a sheet of paper. "This is a clause that states the residents are willing to take full responsibility if anything would happen from taking flying lessons or eating any food that they grew. I want you to have the residents sign this as a show of support and I will personally go before the board."

"I am proud of you, Mr. Dry," Nurse Steal said.

Mr. Dry smiled thinly. "You have been looking very tired, Nurse Steal, don't you think you should take a break?"

"It will pass," she said. "It always has."

That afternoon all the residents gathered in the dayroom and signed the paper, but with little hope or enthusiasm.

"You might get to teach us how to fly again," Rose Merrywood told Harold trying to cheer him up.

"No teach," Harold said shaking his head.

Mr. Fist started flapping his arms, but Harold turned away.

"We want to fly, Harold," Henry Right said. "You have to understand, we need you."

"Oh, dear," Rose Merrywood said.

Harold went to the end of the east wing where the birdbath was. Rose Merrywood joined him. "The birds seem to be happy," Rose Merrywood said.

"Birds always happy," Harold said. "Birds fly. Birds happy."

Rose Merrywood put her hand over his hand. Harold rested his head on her shoulder. Rose Merrywood patted him on the head. "You will have to fly again, Harold," she said. "Not for us, but for yourself. You must always remember we might not have hope for ourselves but we do have hope for you."

"Fly silly. Harold not want to be silly," Harold said, standing and walking away.

"Worthless world," Rose Merrywood mumbled. "You fill us with such promise and then you take it away."

In the late afternoon Nurse Steal gave the paper the residents had signed back to Mr. Dry. "I have an appointment with the board tomorrow," Mr. Dry said. "I have already sent over a copy of the appeal."

"Do you think there is a chance?" Nurse Steal asked.

"I am going to give it my best effort," Mr. Dry said.

"I do hope so," Nurse Steal said. "And all the residents said to tell you good luck and thank you."

"I think you should get a physical, Nurse Steal," Mr. Dry said, looking worried. "You look like you might be more than run down."

"I will give it a thought," she replied, but dismissed the idea. "I am only running on empty," she told herself.

******

"Her toes are long and tapered with red polish on her nails. If you look close enough you can see a tiny white scar on her ankle. Her calves are gently rounded and blend into her knees, which are dimpled," Mr. Fist described the lady.

"Stop, stop," Robert Begone pleaded.

"I'm getting better at this," Mr. Fist smiled.

"What good does it do us?" Jake Lost asked.

Mr. Fist thought for a moment. "I really don't know," he

finally conceded.

"Maybe it is about time we started acting our age," Jake Lost said.

"It is not the same without Paul Mouse," Robert Begone said.

Mr. Fist tore up the picture. "No, it isn't," he agreed. "And I don't think it will ever be."

"We have been good friends," Robert Begone said.

"I could not have made it without you guys," Jake Lost said.

With that, all three men ran toward the door. "Dive, dive," Henry Right shouted as the buzzer sounded.

The aides ran after the men, but they did not have to go far. The three men were standing on the porch hugging each other and laughing although their eyes were filled with tears.

Right after supper Nurse Steal left for home. Driving, she felt dizzy, and once in her apartment she fell into her chair feeling like she would faint. After a few minutes she managed to make it to the bathroom and ran a cool bath. After her bath she felt better and went to bed, falling into a heavy dreamless sleep.

In the morning Mr. Dry went before the board of directors for Rest View, Inc. There were eight men sitting around a large expensive table. All were dressed in suits and ties. Mr. Dry, dressed casually, felt like he was facing a jury that had already found him guilty. Each of the men had a photocopy of Mr. Dry's appeal.

"I am Mr. Springer, president of the company," the man at the head of the table said, and he quickly introduced the other men before he continued. "This matter of yours is highly irregular. Normally our inspectors' decisions are not appealed."

"I thought it best for the welfare of my residents," Mr. Dry said.

"You must understand that we have to be very careful in the way we manage our holdings," Mr. Springer said. "The slightest mistake and we can be hauled into court and sued."

"I understand," Mr. Dry said. "I have a waiver with me the residents have signed that they understand the ramifications and will take full responsibility for their actions?"

"Surely you know that a waiver is merely a piece of paper that can be ripped to shreds in a court of law," another man at the table said.

"Don't you think that human needs should take precedence over the law?" Mr. Dry asked, knowing the man who had answered his question was an attorney.

"I must tell you I see nothing wrong with a garden or these so called flying lessons," Mr. Springer said. "We all fantasize, but, no matter what I feel, there is no way we can go above what the lawyers tell us. I am sorry."

"I hope you all live to be one hundred and have to live in one of your own homes," Mr. Dry said and walked out.

"Mr. Dry should be fired for insubordination," one of the men said angrily to Mr. Springer.

The others nodded their heads.

"Should I fire a man for feeling for his people?" Mr. Springer asked.

Nobody answered.

"That is what I thought," Mr. Springer said, "and let us hope none of us have to spend our last days in a rest home."

When Mr. Dry got back to Rest View Nurse Steal knew by his look he had not been successful, but she was proud of him for trying.

At lunch, Mr. Dry addressed the residents. "They said no," he said simply.

"We figured," Mr. Fist said.

"We could all go on a hunger strike," Robert Begone said.

"We wouldn't last two days," Jake Lost said.

"Thank you for trying," Martha Dearheart said.

"It was the least I could do," Mr. Dry said.

No one else said anything. What was there to say?

Nurse Steal suddenly felt weary. Her legs grew weak and she felt hot and it was hard to breathe. She started to pick up a tray when an excruciating pain shot through her chest and with a dreadful cry she collapsed to the floor.

"Call an ambulance," Mr. Dry shouted to an aide as he rushed to Nurse Steal.

Harold ran over and picked up Nurse Steal's hand. "No, no," he cried. "Nurse Steal fly, Harold teach. No, no."

All the residents watched the ambulance pull away. Harold, with tears streaming from his eyes, repeated over and over again, "Harold love Nurse Steal, Harold love Nurse Steal."

It was almost dark when the residents were called to the dayroom. Mr. Dry, ashen, and with an unsteady voice said, "Twenty minutes ago Nurse Steal passed away. Her heart gave out. We will all miss her. She was a caring person and she loved all of you."

Harold ran to his room and throwing himself on the bed he cried, "Nurse Steal fly now, Nurse Steal angel."

The residents all went somberly to their rooms.

Grace Brethren's hands were clasped in prayer, "Dear God, those in life who spend their hours in service for others, take them into your fold and give them the peace and love they searched for, and in all your graciousness, forgive those that hurt others."

Rose Merrywood sighed. "Now we have nothing. No nurse that loves us, no garden and no flying lessons."

Bertha Shields was holding Randolph. "I will never die. You must not fear. I will never leave you," she told the teddy bear.

Mr. Fist tore the pages out of the *Playboy*. Then ripping them into smaller pieces, he tossed them in the garbage can.

Robert Begone took the four pair of shoes from under his bed and set them in the hall.

Jake Lost turned off his hearing aid and tried not to feel.

Martha Dearheart held the pearl pin in her hand and said, "Dear, dear, Nurse Steal. I hope you knew how much we loved and needed you."

******

It was ten o'clock at night. Harold was in bed with his eyes shut, but he was not sleeping. The face of Nurse Steal appeared in his mind. Her face was filled with longing. "Go away, go away," Harold pleaded.

But the face did not go away and the image said tenderly,

"Teach them how to fly."

"No fly, no hope, no love," Harold said, squeezing his eyelids shut as tight as he could.

"You must teach them," Nurse Steal's face pleaded.

"No, no," Harold moaned, opening his eyes and sitting up.

Nurse Steal's vision did not go away. "You must," Nurse Steal beckoned. "You must teach them."

Harold put on his bib overalls. "Harold love Nurse Steal," he said. "Harold hope for Nurse Steal."

"Fa, La, La," drifted through the window. The little brown bird with red eyes was on the window sill looking in.

"No fly," Harold said shaking his head.

"Fa, La, La," the bird sang louder.

"Fly, fly," Nurse Steal said.

"No fly," Harold said.

"Fly for me," Nurse Steal's image said.

"Fa, La, La," drifted even louder through the window.

"They hope," Nurse Steal's voice whispered in Harold's ears. "You must trust me. They hope."

"Fa, La, La," the bird sang.

"No, no, Harold too sad," Harold said.

The little brown bird with the red eyes flew away.

Harold paced back and forth in his room.

<h1 align="center">Chapter Eleven</h1>

It was ten at night and Hazel was in the kitchen making a cup of coffee. Harold poked his head around the corner of his room. Not seeing anyone, he hurried to Rose Merrywood's room. "I am glad you came over. I am lonely tonight," Rose Merrywood said.

"Up, up," Harold urged, quickly moving her wheelchair to the edge of the bed.

"What are we doing?" Rose Merrywood asked.

"Fly," Harold said. "We fly."

Harold helped Rose Merrywood into the chair. "Oh, this is exciting," she said.

"Go birdbath," Harold instructed her.

Rose Merrywood wheeled toward the end of the wing.

Next, Harold ran to Martha Dearheart's room. Harold grasped her by the hand and implored. "Hope, hope, must hope."

"Harold, go back to bed," Martha Dearheart scolded just as Rose Merrywood wheeled past her door.

"Birdbath, birdbath," Harold said.

Martha Dearheart got out of bed and put on her robe. "Oh, all right. I can't sleep anyway," she said.

Mr. Fist, hearing the noise, went out into the hall. Seeing

Rose Merrywood and Martha Dearheart, he went to Robert Begone's room. "Get up," he told him.

Robert Begone sat up in bed. "Come on," Mr. Fist said. "There's a party at the end of the hall."

"Do they have dancing girls?" Robert Begone asked.

"Grace Brethren is running around topless," Mr. Fist said.

Robert Begone sprang out of bed.

Robert Begone and Mr. Fist shook Jake Lost awake. He did not have his hearing aid on and they took him by the arms and escorted him down the hall. "What? What?" Jake Lost kept asking.

"Who cares what," Robert Begone answered. "Hurry up before Grace comes to her senses."

After Jake Lost was with Rose Merrywood and Martha Dearheart Harold told Mr. Fist and Robert Begone, "We fly, we fly. Go get other people."

Robert Begone gave Mr. First a dirty look. "So I lied," Mr. Fist said.

"We bust out of this joint tonight," Robert Begone told Mr. Fist as they hurried down the hall to wake up other residents.

Soon Bertha Shields and Randolph, Wilma Happy, Betty Frost, Gloria Sane, Henry Right, George Early, and Letha Johnston and Carrie had joined the group.

Harold opened the window as far as he could and started flapping his arms up and down slowly. "Nurse Steal say all hope. Nurse Steal say all fly," he said with deep sadness in his voice, but in the sadness was a great resolve that touched each person.

"For Nurse Steal, we can all hope," Mr. Fist said, flapping his arms.

"We can all fly," all the people shouted in unison and started flapping their arms.

"Bird say must hope," Harold said. "Bird sing and teach fly."

"Wait, we have to get Grace Brethren," Martha Dearheart said and rushed to Grace Brethren's room.

Grace Brethren was asleep with her Bible clutched firmly in her hands. Martha Dearheart shook her gently. "Grace, Grace, you have to get up. Harold is giving a late night flying lesson and I think tonight we will really fly."

"Go away," Grace Brethren said. "I want to sleep. You know I don't want to fly."

"Come on, please?" Martha Dearheart implored.

"No," Grace Brethren said firmly.

"Oh, Grace, you will miss us, "Martha Dearheart said.

Martha Dearheart hurried back to the group. "She does not want to come," she said.

"For Nurse Steal we hope and fly," Harold said.

"Fa, La, La," he sang, flapping his arms faster.

"Fa, La, La," the others sang, also flapping their arms faster.

The flapped and flapped but nothing happened.

They flapped more but still nothing.

They flapped and started to grow tired.

Harold turned and looked beseechingly at the birdbath.

"Fa, La, La," Harold sang.

"Fa, La, La," the others sang.

There was no reply from outside.

Harold put his face close to the window, "Please, please, not for Harold but for Harold's friends and Nurse Steal. Fa, La, La."

There was no reply.

"Please, please? Fa, La, La," Harold pleaded.

There was no reply.

"Please?"

There was no reply.

Harold turned from the window and let his arms fall dejectedly to his sides.

The people, exhausted, stopped flapping and a silent gloom settled over them. Tears streamed down Harold's cheeks. There was nothing he could say. Rose Merrywood started sobbing. Martha Dearheart, touching the pearl pin on her nightgown sadly, turned toward her room. Henry Right said softly, "I flew an inch once."

"It is no use, Harold," Mr. Fist said. "Even if we think we hope, we do not truly have hope."

"We are all so sorry," Wilma Happy said.

Martha Dearheart had taken several steps when the others started toward their rooms.

"Fa, La, La," a bird sang from outside as softly as a single raindrop hitting a leaf.

The people all froze in place, as if the song from the bird put them in a trance. Harold put his ear to the window.

"Fa, La, La," the bird sang no louder than a child's whispered secret.

"Fa, La, La," Harold sang softly.

"Fa, La, La," the bird sang louder.

"Hope, dream, proud to be old," Harold hollered at the top of his lungs and flapping his arms furiously.

"Damn right," Mr. Fist yelled.

"Fa, La, La," the residents sang, flapping their arms again.

"Fa, La, La," the bird sang as clear as a church bell.

Harold started flapping his arms as fast as he could. "Fly, fly," he beckoned.

Mr. Fist's arms were a blur.

"Fa, La, La," the bird sang.

"Hope, hope, we all hope," Harold called happily.

"We love you, Nurse Steal," Martha Dearheart called..

"Fa, La, La," the bird sang.

"We can do it," George Early yelled.

Hazel, leaving the kitchen, heard the noise from the end of the east wing. Turning the corner of the dayroom she saw the residents at the end of the hall. "What are you doing?" she demanded and ran towards the residents.

"Fa, La, La," Harold sang.

"Fa, La, La," the people sang.

"Fa, La, La," the bird sang.

Grace Brethren came out of her room. "Wait for me, wait for me. Please wait for me. I don't want to be alone."

Hazel and the aide ran toward the residents. "Stop whatever you are doing," Hazel ordered.

Grace Brethren called, "Wait, wait, please wait."

"Fa, La, La," the bird sang.

Harold's feet came off the ground. "Hope, hope, fly, fly,"

he called.

"I told you," Henry Right yelled.

The people's arms started to beat as one. "We hope, we all hope," Mr. Fist huffed.

"Wait for me," Grace Brethren cried, now no more than ten yards from the group, with Hazel only a few steps behind her.

With one more flap the people rose from the floor. For a brief instant they looked at each other in astonishment and then suddenly they vanished to be replaced by a host of small drab brown birds, each with a small swath of varying colors on their breast - one had a splash of blue. They circled around Grace Brethren and Hazel, each chirping goodbye and well wishes before flying out the window.

"Why didn't I believe?" Grace Brethren beseeched Hazel.

Hazel was speechless.

Randolph and the Raggedy Ann doll, wrapped in each other's arms, were in a wheelchair gazing vacantly out the window.

The host of birds lit in an oak tree and chirped happily to each other. A small brown bird with mysterious red eyes watched them silently for a few moments before flying away to never return. One bird, with a white breast and a pearl pin in its beak, guided by starlight, hopped around the tree until it found a small crevice and carefully poked the pearl pin into the safety of the tree.

Chapter Twelve

Fall had returned. The trees at the base of the hill were brilliant reds and yellows. The grass was turning brown. A woman had permission from Mr. Dry to sit outside by the bird bath by herself. Nurse Cole would unlock the doors for her and wedge one open so the lady could come back inside easily.

The lady was sitting on a bench that had been placed close to the birdbath - next to her were a tattered brown teddy bear and a Raggedy Ann doll. "Randolph and Carrie, you children must never steal. It only causes pain for everybody," she said to the dolls. From her dress pocket the woman removed a small garnet pin. Holding the pin up to the sky, she admired the red brilliance of the stone. She placed the pin gently on the edge of the birdbath like she had done many times before.

A small host of little brown birds with a splash of varying colors on their breasts flew around Rest View and landed in a redbud tree outside the window of one of the rooms. An old man smiled at the birds and moved his arms up and down like they were wings.

"Fa, La, La," a brown bird with a splash of blue on its breast sang.

"Fa, La, La," the man sang back.

A single bird flew away from the other birds, circled Rest View, and landed on the edge of the birdbath. Seeing the garnet pin it seemed to sigh.

Picking up the pin tenderly in its beak the bird flew away, hesitated and started to turn back around, but changed its mind and continued on. It flew to an oak tree where several months earlier it had hidden a pearl pin. Putting both the pearl and garnet pin in its beak it flew back to the birdbath. The bird circled the lady several times before landing next to her hand.

"I meant no harm. Please believe me?" the lady said.

The bird pecked gently at the lady's hand until she held out her hand palm up. The bird carefully placed the pearl and garnet pins in the lady's palm, "Fa, La, La," it sang happily, and flew back to its friends.

"Oh children," Grace Brethren sighed to the teddy bear and the Raggedy Ann doll.

She closed her hand tenderly around the pearl and garnet pins and felt a soothing sense of relief from the gift of forgiveness.

THE END